MARVELOUS MARK
and His
NO-GOOD DOG

Heather Grovet

FR

REVIEW AND HERALD® PUBLISHING ASSOCIATION
HAGERSTOWN, MD 21740

The author assumes full responsibility for the accuracy of all facts and
quotations as cited in this book.

This book was
Edited by Jeannette R. Johnson
Designed by Tina Ivany
Cover illustration by Ron Bell
Cover design by Pierce Creative/Matt Pierce
Typeset: 13/16 Goudy Old Style

PRINTED IN U.S.A.

07 06 05 04 03   5 4 3 2 1

R&H Cataloging Service
Grovet, Heather Marie, 1963-
    Marvelous Mark and his no-good dog.

    I. Title.

                    813.6

ISBN 0-8280-1734-4

Other books by Heather Grovet:

Petunia, the Ugly Pug
Prince Prances Again
Prince, the Persnickety Pony
Sarah Lee and Maybe the Mule

To order, call 1-800-765-6955.

Visit us at www.reviewandherald.com for information on other
Review and Herald® products.

Dedication

To Bernard and Nadine
Great in-laws—and great neighbors, too!

Contents

1

Marvelous Mark Strikes Out

Dear God, this has started out to be another horrible day in the middle of a horrible week. Actually, the past few months have been horrible, too, but since I'm not a complainer I won't bore You with the details of my life.

I'm sure You already know everything anyhow. My life is terrible. I don't have a single friend since we've moved. At my old school I was popular. I was funny. Everyone talked to me and laughed at my jokes.

No one likes me at my new school. No one laughs at my jokes. They don't even seem to notice that I'm alive.

What should I do, God? Even my family's driving me crazy. My dad's busy all the time, my mom's frazzled, my baby brother, Ryan— Let's not even mention Ryan! And Grandpa Olsen is the worst one of them all.

"You're going to be late," Grandpa Olsen suddenly barked at my dad. "Again."

7

Dad glanced at his watch, then shifted the half-ton down a gear. "We're almost there," Dad said. He wasn't smiling.

Grandpa had a stroke a few months ago. He's been in the local hospital ever since then. He used to be a pretty cool guy before his stroke. I spent most of my summers on Grandpa's farm swimming in the river, throwing a base-ball back and forth with Grandpa, and just generally having fun. But a few months ago, not long after I started grade five, my Grandpa had a stroke. For a while everyone thought he was going to die. He couldn't talk, he wouldn't eat, and his right arm and leg didn't work.

My dad spent most of November at the hospital, trying to help Grandpa. And something must have worked, because Grandpa didn't die. He began to eat, and then talk, and slowly his hand began to move. But Grandpa's leg is still bad. He can't even walk a step or two, and that makes him mad.

And when Grandpa's mad, we all know about it.

Dad finally pulled into an enormous farmyard. He drove the truck carefully past a white two-story farm-house and back to the barnyard. Mile after mile of corrals were back by the barn, and each pen was filled with bawling herds of cattle.

Dad parked the truck and slipped out.

I sighed and opened the truck door.

"Boy!" Grandpa Olsen's voice was sharp. "Don't you have any sense? Put a hat on before you freeze your ears!"

You see? My grandpa has become the world's biggest grump.

I pulled a knit hat over my short brown hair and tried to smile at Grandpa. Even though I hadn't been a Christian very long—maybe only a year or so—I did know that Christians are supposed to be kind and patient to old people. Especially old grandpas. So I bit my lip for the hundredth time that day and tried to be pleasant.

"There," I said. "I put my hat on, Grandpa."

"Good," Grandpa Olsen said. "It covers your messy hair."

Now that hurt! I'd always thought my hair was one of my better features. I know that 11-year-old boys aren't supposed to worry about their looks that much, but sometimes I can't help but notice myself in the mirror. I'm kind of tall and gangly. Dad says I'm going to be big, like Grandpa and him, but right now I'm in that weird in-between stage. My ears stick out too far on the sides of my head. My nose seems a bit crooked. On the side of my face I have a mole that I don't like very much.

But my hair? I had always thought my hair looked good. It's thick and has a slight wave, and it's a nice, rich dark-brown color.

I wondered if Grandpa had looked in the mirror lately. He's let his hair get long and wild. A piece hangs in his eyes half the time, and some days he doesn't even bother to shave. He really has no business complaining about my hair!

I opened my mouth to say something, and then closed it again.

That wasn't easy for me. My best friend in Calgary has a nickname for me: Marvelous Mark Olsen and the Mighty Moving Mouth. That should tell you a little something about my ability to talk. Talking is my game, and being quiet drives me insane.

Dad was already standing outside the truck. He beckoned at us with one hand. "Come on," he called. "We're late."

"You're always late," Grandpa grumbled.

I smiled weakly at Grandpa and slid off the truck seat.

"Careful," Dad warned. "The ground's icy here."

I zipped up my winter coat and pulled the hat down around my ears a bit farther. It was the coldest day in January, and my dad chooses this day to come pick up our new cows. I never could understand grown-ups!

Dad looked in at Grandpa. "Would you please come with us, Father?" he asked. "I could use your advice."

Grandpa shook his head stubbornly.

"Please," Dad begged.

"You know I can't walk," Grandpa said sharply.

"I could push you in the wheelchair," Dad said.

Grandpa pursed his lips. "Over the frozen cow patties?" he scoffed. "I don't think so. Leave me alone."

Dad stared at Grandpa. Grandpa stared back at him and frowned. "And shut the truck door," he snapped. "I'm going to freeze to death in here."

Dad sighed. "There is a heater in the truck," he said. "Turn it on." He shut the door softly, and then looked at me. "OK, Mark," he said. "I guess it's just the two of us."

I didn't say anything until we were some distance from the truck. And even when I did speak I kept my voice quiet so Grandpa couldn't hear me.

"Why does he have to act like that?" I asked.

Dad was quiet for a moment. "I don't know," he finally said. "I think he's depressed."

"*He's* depressed!" I said sharply. "I'm the one that should be depressed. Just being around him makes me miserable."

"Grandpa was always an outdoor man," Dad explained. "And now he's had a stroke. I don't think he wants to live if he can't walk and do the things he enjoys doing."

"So he wants to make everyone around him miserable?" I asked.

Dad shrugged. "Maybe so," he said. "Yesterday I got up my courage and tried to tell him that God loves him and has a plan for his life."

"You're kidding!" I exclaimed. "What did he say?"

Grandpa Olsen had never been a Christian, even when life had been going well for him. My mom and dad had become Seventh-day Adventists about two years before after attending some meetings. Grandpa had been polite when they'd tried to talk to him about Christianity, but even then he hadn't been interested.

11

I could imagine how he'd act now, when he was so nasty all the time.

"It didn't go very well," Dad admitted. "He called me a religious freak, and some other names that I won't repeat, and told me to shut up."

"I'm shocked," I said sarcastically. "Totally shocked."

"Mark," Dad warned with a frown.

"Well, come on, Dad," I said, "I have a feeling that Grandpa's problems are too big for anyone, even God."

"Nothing's too difficult for God," Dad said.

"I guess we'll see."

"We need to give him time," Dad said stoutly. "Time and prayer, that will be the answer."

I didn't imagine Grandpa would be the one doing the praying, either.

"Hello!" a loud voice called from across the yard.

I looked up to see a tall man striding toward us. His face was lined and wrinkled, but he moved briskly. The man raised one hand to wave at us, and then waved toward Grandpa, who was still sitting inside the truck. I saw Grandpa turn away without waving back.

"Here comes Mr. McGinness," Dad said.

The McGinness Ranch was famous for its Simmental cattle herd. That's why we drove here today with our truck and stock trailer. Dad had arranged to buy 10 heifers (young cows that hadn't calved yet) from Mr. McGinness.

Grandpa Olsen had owned cattle a few years ago, and some horses, too. Now he said he wanted nothing to do with livestock. "Just a lot of work," he had grumbled as we drove to the McGinness Ranch. "And I don't want to see them."

"Come to pick up your lassies, hey there, young man?" Mr. McGinness asked cheerfully. "I've got them a-waiting for you."

Mr. McGinness was one of the tallest men I had ever seen, with big teeth like a horse. His head was bare, and his ears were red under a mop of wild gray hair. But he seemed perfectly comfortable standing there in the cold.

I hesitated. "We came for some cows, Mr. McGinness," I finally said doubtfully. "Not lassies."

Mr. McGinness laughed loudly. "Aye," he chuckled. "A lassie is a girl, and I do believe that your father is wanting cows. That's the only way I know of to get calves this spring!"

I flushed and nodded my head. I should have kept my mouth shut, I guess. That's one of my biggest faults. I talk too much. But I guess I've already told you that. You know—Marvelous Mark and the Mighty Moving Mouth.

"Come on, ol' chap," Mr. McGinness said. "I'll show the beasts to you. Ten fine heifers, ready to calve in a few months."

We stopped at the edge of a high wooden corral. Mr. McGinness scrambled up the fence as easily as a young man, with my dad and I following.

He pointed at a small herd of cattle that huddled

together at the far end of the small corral. "There ye be," he said. "Ready and waiting."

"Excellent," Dad said. "I suppose I should pull my stock trailer up to the chute."

"Indeed!" Mr. McGinness agreed. "We should have done that at the start."

"Sorry," Dad said. "But I was running a bit late."

"Your dad was never late," Mr. McGinness said. "I thought you'd be a chip off the ol' block."

"Would a chip off the block be a blockhead?" Dad asked with a cheerful grin.

Mr. McGinness laughed and slapped Dad on the back. "Ha!" he chuckled. "Now that sounds more like an Olsen. Always joking around and all."

I couldn't imagine my grandpa joking anymore, but I supposed it was possible. When pigs flew, maybe.

"Now," Mr. McGinness continued, "pull your truck over there by the chute. I'll get my men to help me bring the cattle across the alley to you."

I watched as my father turned around and headed back for the half-ton and stock trailer.

I hoped Mr. McGinness wouldn't want me to climb in the corral and help him chase the cows. I'm a city kid, after all. I mean, I've lived on the farm for only a month, and I haven't had anything to do with cattle yet. But I'm 11 years old, which means that I'm supposed to be brave, so I tried to act casual while studying those incredibly big and ugly cows.

Mr. McGinness put his fingers to his lips and blew

a loud whistle that made me jump so high I almost shot out of my heavy winter boots.

"Now, young man," Mr. McGinness said, his face beaming happily. "My men will bring your cows in."

In a moment three black-and-white dogs raced across the frozen yard toward Mr. McGinness. I raised my eyebrows. I had been expecting people—men—to help Mr. McGinness, but this was even better. I don't like cows very much, but I've always been crazy about dogs.

The three dogs stopped in front of Mr. McGinness, their tails wagging wildly.

Mr. McGinness wasn't smiling anymore. "What are you doing here?" he asked in a gruff voice. He waved a hand at the smallest of the three dogs.

The little dog waved the plume of his tail cheerfully.

"What kind of dogs are they?" I asked.

The little dog stood up when he heard my voice and trotted over to the edge of the fence. I slid down and began to stroke the dog's soft back. His tail wagged faster now. He closed his eyes in bliss and curled his lips back, almost as though he was smiling.

"They're Border collies," Mr. McGinness said. "The best sheep dogs in the world. And the best cattle dogs, too." He frowned at the smallest dog. "Except for that one," he said.

I studied the dogs. At first glance they had all looked identical, almost like triplets—coal black, with white legs and white ruffs around their necks. But as I looked at them carefully I began to see some differences.

The small dog, the one that I was petting, was the prettiest one. He had a perfect white blaze down the front of his face, and his ears stood upright eagerly. He had a happy expression, like the sort of person who went around all day smiling.

The other dogs were handsome, too, but not half as handsome as the little one.

"What's his name?" I asked Mr. McGinness.

"That's Jet," Mr. McGinness grunted.

As I continued to pet Jet I became aware of a strange sound coming from the little dog. It had started off as a quiet hum but had grown louder and louder until now it was the beginning of a soft growl.

I quickly glanced down at the dog. He beamed up at me, his tail wagging happily, and growled again.

I raised my hand and counted my fingers. Nope; none of them were missing! Jet seemed perfectly happy except for the horrible growl that was now coming between his smiling black lips.

"Ignore the daft beast," Mr. McGinness said, glaring from the fence at Jet. "He's a fine one for growling when he's happy. His ma was the same way. Scared people sometimes."

I sighed with relief and put my hand back on Jet's head. "He's beautiful," I said.

Jet wagged his tail again, smiling up at me with bright brown eyes.

"Beauty is as beauty does." Mr. McGinness

frowned. "He's naught but a worthless pup." He glared at the little dog. "Jet, lie down."

The dog's ears drooped a bit, and he pressed harder against me.

Mr. McGinness raised one hand slightly. "Jet, down," he ordered sharply.

The small dog sighed, then laid down on the ice by my feet. His tail still wagged slowly back and forth.

I looked down at the little dog. *I wonder why Mr. McGinness doesn't like Jet,* I thought with a faint frown. *Anyone who likes Marvelous Mark (as this dog obviously does) has to be pretty special! Especially now, when friends are in seriously short supply.*

2

The McGinness Dogs

Now, young man," Mr. McGinness said. "If you stand there quietly I'll show you a thing or two." With one last glare at the little dog Mr. McGinness climbed over the wooden fence and into the corral. He walked to the left and swung open a big gate.

"Now watch this," he said. "A good cattle dog is worth its weight in gold." The man motioned toward the herd of cattle that stood at the back of the corral. "Tippy . . . Floss," the man called. "Come by."

The two larger dogs sprang to their feet and slipped under the fence. They galloped around the herd of cows, moving clockwise until they were behind the group.

"Down!" Mr. McGinness called.

Both dogs dropped to their bellies in the straw. Their eyes remained focused on the group of cows.

"What do you want them to do?" I asked, watching the dogs with amazement.

"They're going to take your cattle out of this pen and move them down the alleyway," Mr. McGinness said, pointing to the left. "Then we'll load them in your stock trailer."

"Don't you need some help?" I asked. *Please don't ask me*, I thought, looking at the cows. *I'd rather have bamboo shoots stuck under my fingernails. I'd rather take a trip to the dentist. I'd rather kiss a girl— Oh, yuck! I wouldn't go that far. But you get the point.*

The heifers had unfriendly expressions on their faces, and they seemed to have grown even bigger, right in front of me.

Mr. McGinness grinned. "Nay, lad," he said. "My men will be all the help we'll need." He turned to face the cattle and the two dogs that were still crouched on the ground. "Walk up!" Mr. McGinness ordered.

The two dogs rose together and stepped toward the cows. The 10 heifers backed up a few steps, then turned to face the dogs. The biggest cow, who was the size of a bulldozer or maybe a small house, lowered her head and shook it at the dogs. One of the dogs barked, showing a mouthful of sharp white teeth.

That dog obviously isn't too bright, I thought, comparing the 30-pound dog to the enormous cow. *Chasing that cow would be like me trying to kill a Tyrannosaurus rex with a bottle of mosquito spray.*

The big red cow pawed the ground. A shower of frozen snow sprayed behind her, and she snorted sharply.

"Ah, that lassie has a bad attitude," Mr. McGinness

observed. "You'll have to watch her, young man. Especially after she has her calf this spring."

"Is she mean?" I asked.

Mr. McGinness didn't answer. He didn't have to. Even dumb city boys like me can tell a nasty cow when they see one.

Mr. McGinness didn't look worried. He frowned at the red cow and waved a hand toward the herd. "Walk up!" Mr. McGinness ordered the dogs again.

Both dogs sprang forward. The red cow lowered her head and waved it back and forth. She had a wide forehead, perfect for grinding dogs or boys into the ground, I imagined, and angry narrow eyes.

I've seen cartoons of Satan. They show him dressed in red, with horns on his head. Well, now I know where the artists got that idea about Satan. They had probably seen this cow! How could Mr. McGinness expect those little dogs to chase that cow?

The red cow snorted and rushed forward, swinging her head at the dogs.

"Holy cow!" I yelled. "Watch out!"

Maybe I should have said "unholy cow," because she certainly acted more like a lion than a Christian!

The dogs didn't flinch. In fact, one of them sprang forward, straight at the cow's head. I didn't want to look, and closed my eyes quickly.

There was a loud bellow.

I opened my eyes.

The red cow had turned away from the dogs and

was galloping across the corral, kicking her feet behind her. A streak of blood showed on the end of her nose. One of the dogs hung casually from her tail, looking for all the world like a kite on the end of a string. He bobbed up and down with every stride the cow took, his feet totally off the ground.

The rest of the herd bellowed wildly and charged after their leader, the second Border collie on their heels. In a few minutes the entire group was in the other corral, pressed against the far wall.

"That'll teach that lassie," Mr. McGinness said. "She'll be a bit more respectful next time!"

I wondered how many teeth the dog lost doing that tail hanging trick. He was now back on the ground, standing near the fence beside the other dog. Mr. McGinness continued to call out orders to the two dogs, and before long the herd was loaded in the back of our stock trailer.

When they were finished, Mr. McGinness smiled broadly. "Good lads!" he called approvingly. "Leave it."

He seemed to have totally forgotten the small dog that was still lying quietly by my feet. But at his command to leave it, the little dog got up and pressed his face against my hand.

"That was incredible!" I said. "Can Jet do that?" I ruffled Jet's silky black ears.

Mr. McGinness grunted. "Ha," he snorted. " 'Tis a poor dog indeed, and I'll not be having him on the farm for long. Won't work the cattle at all."

"Is he scared of cows?" I asked.

Mr. McGinness shook his head. "Nay, son," he said. "Not scared. Just addle-headed."

I must have looked confused, because Mr. McGinness explained what he meant.

"He's foolish. Daft."

"He's stupid?" I asked. It seemed to me that any dog that wouldn't chase those enormous cows was pretty smart!

"I wouldn't call him stupid," Mr. McGinness said. "But he'd rather play than work. He spends all his time chasing birds and such."

"He's not chasing birds now," I pointed out.

"Nay, young man," Mr. McGinness said. "About the only thing he likes better than birds are people. He lays around all day wantin' his belly scratched while the other dogs do all the work."

"He's still young," I said. "Maybe he'll be better when he grows up."

"No," Mr. McGinness said firmly. "Either a pup has the urge to work or he doesn't. And this one doesn't."

"What are you going to do with him?" I asked. I glanced anxiously at the dog who was now dancing merrily in the snow nearby.

"I'm not a heartless beast," Mr. McGinness said. "I'll find him another home where he can be their pet, and not a real worker."

Mr. McGinness suddenly seemed to see me with new

eyes. "Aye, now," he said slowly. "I have a wee idea."

Father scrambled from behind the stock trailer. "I've got the door shut," he said. "So I guess we're ready to go, Mark."

"There's just the matter of my check, ol' chap," Mr. McGinness said quickly.

"Of course," Dad assured him. "I have my checkbook in the truck."

"Robert," Mr. McGinness said slowly, "you wouldn't be wanting a dog, now, would you?"

My dad's eyebrows shot up so high they disappeared under his hat. "A dog?" he said incredulously. "Never! I hate dogs."

"Dad!" I exclaimed. "You don't hate dogs."

"I do," Dad said, nodding his head briskly. "And your mother does, too."

"She does not!" I protested loudly. "And you know it. Why, just last year she was begging for a little house dog."

"That was before your brother was born," Dad said.

"She quit liking dogs when she had the baby?" I asked with a wicked grin.

"You know what I mean," Dad said. "She's too busy now."

"Maybe we should get rid of Ryan," I said. "That would make things a lot easier."

Dad sighed and turned to Mr. McGinness. "My poor wife's in quite a flap," he said. "We moved into our new house at Christmas time, and there are still boxes laying around everywhere. And our Christmas tree's still up, standing in the middle of all the other junk."

"It's the end of January," Mr. McGinness commented.

"Maybe she's waiting for Ukrainian Christmas," I suggested.

"Ukrainian Christmas is over," Dad said. "And anyway, I don't think you could convince anyone that we're Ukrainian with a name like Olsen."

"I don't care what we are," I said. "I want a dog."

"We don't have time for a dog," Dad argued.

But I could tell he was weakening. This was the time for Marvelous Mark to move in for the kill. All's fair in love and war, and I already loved Jet.

"I have time for a dog," I said quietly. "I have plenty of time. After all, no one comes over to play anymore since I don't have any friends. I have no one."

"Mark!"

"I need this dog," I said desperately. "Then I'd have at least one friend in the world."

Dad groaned and put his hands to his head. "Give it a rest, Mark," he said. "Things aren't that bad."

"Yes, they are," I said. I put a miserable look on my face.

Dad rolled his eyes and looked away from me.

"Why did you move back here?" Mr. McGinness asked.

"My dad had a stroke a few months ago," Dad said. "He's going to need someone to help take care of him when he gets out of the hospital."

"I'd heard that he was ill," Mr. McGinness said. He gestured to the truck parked nearby.

"He's on the mend," Dad said. "We're hoping that he can move in with us before long."

Move in with us! I hadn't heard that one before! Now wouldn't that be just great! Grandpa Olsen, the champion grouch, living in the same house with me. Now I was really depressed.

"He's not going back to his own house?" Mr. McGinness asked.

Dad shook his head. "He has a lot of stairs in his house, and he'll never manage to get up them," Dad explained. "And anyway the house is getting old."

"Aye; aren't we all?" Mr. McGinness chuckled.

"I'm not getting old," I told the men. "And I want Jet. Please."

"We don't even have a doghouse," Dad said.

"I'll build one," I said.

Dad laughed. "You didn't even finish the Lego house you started over Christmas," he said. "How could you ever build a real dog house?"

"It would teach me responsibility," I said. "You know how important that is for a kid my age."

Dad grinned, and his eyes twinkled. "My son, the lawyer," he said, looking at Mr. McGinness. "Mark would win every case by wearing the judge down. Or maybe he'll be a salesman. This boy could sell an Eskimo an igloo!"

"Please, Dad!" I begged.

Jet seemed to be begging, too. His tail wagged wildly as he looked from face to face, trying to follow our conversation.

Mr. McGinness spoke up. "He's out of Floss, here, and Fly, another of my dogs, who you haven't met yet. He should cost a pretty penny, but I won't charge you a thing. I just want him off the place."

"But I don't like dogs," Dad said.

"But I do!"

Dad gave me a long, hard look. "OK," he said slowly. "You have a deal, Mr. McGinness. I'll take the 10 heifers if you throw in one cattle dog."

Mr. McGinness shook his head. "Ten heifers," he corrected, "and one worthless, no-good dog. Just be certain that you don't let anyone know where you got him."

I bent over and slapped my knee, an enormous grin on my face. Jet dashed over and tried to lick my cheek.

"You're not worthless," I whispered fiercely in the little dog's ear. "And you're going to come home with me!"

Jet seemed pleased with the deal. He barked once, and then began to spin around, trying to catch his tail in his mouth.

Dad smiled, but Mr. McGinness just shook his head. "He's a fool dog," he grumbled sourly. "And he'll never amount to anything much."

3

Jet
Comes Home

The cab of the truck was crowded now. Both Dad and Grandpa are big men, and it was a tight fit with the three of us on the truck seat. Jet made things even tighter, and I couldn't help noticing that he smelled bad. Like a cow, I suppose.

Mr. McGinness peered in the window and smiled a crooked smile at us. "Now, young man," he said, looking at me, "ya take good care of your dog, ya hear?"

"I will," I promised.

"He's going to have a touch of nerves," Mr. McGinness continued. "Never been in no truck before."

Dad glanced at the dog and tightened his lips. I could tell it wasn't really nerves he was worrying about. "I hope he won't piddle on the floor," he said.

"Nay," Mr. McGinness snorted. "I can promise ya he won't mess in your vehicle."

"But will Jet promise the same thing?" Dad retorted.

"An' he's never been in a house, either," Mr.

McGinness went on, ignoring Dad. "So make sure ya take things slow, young man. Give 'im time to settle in."

"I'll be a good dog owner," I promised.

"Get your grandpa here to help ya if ya have problems," Mr. McGinness advised. "He knows a thing or two about dogs an' such."

Grandpa stared straight ahead, not once looking at Mr. McGinness.

"Thanks for all your help," Dad said. "We better get going. I'd like to be home before it gets dark."

"Off with you, then!" Mr. McGinness said. He stepped back from the truck and nodded his head.

Dad rolled the window up, then shifted the half-ton into gear. In a moment we were rolling down the farm lane. The road was rough with frozen ruts and mud lumps, and each lurch of the vehicle seemed to almost knock Jet off his feet. The little dog's tail had lowered from its cheerful position and now hung limply.

"Don't be scared," I told the dog. "I'll take care of you."

Jet staggered as Dad turned from the lane onto the main road, then caught his balance.

"You needn't drive so fast," Grandpa Olsen said crossly, glancing at the dog.

"I'm *not* speeding," Dad said.

"Well, you're driving awfully fast for someone who's hauling a load of cows," Grandpa said. "An expensive load of cows, too, I'm thinking."

Dad sighed and slowed down a bit. "There," he said. "Is that better?"

Grandpa only grunted.

Jet pushed his face against my leg. He was panting in the warmth of the vehicle, and his brow was wrinkled like that of a worried old man. I scratched the dog's back, and he thumped his tail once against the truck floor before crowding even closer to me.

"I think Jet's nervous," I said.

"I'm a bit nervous, too," Dad said with a grin. "What's your mother going to say when I bring a pup home?"

"If she's smart she'll tell you to take the dog back," Grandpa snapped. "You people don't know anything about dogs."

"I've read a lot of books about dogs," I said.

"Ha!" Grandpa snorted. "Books. A lot of good that will do."

"Do you hate dogs, too?" I asked Grandpa.

Grandpa didn't say anything.

"Jet's a good dog," I promised the men. "And we'll be fine."

"He's going to be trouble," Grandpa predicted. "Border collies are always trouble. He'll chase cars. He'll chase the cows. He'll bark all night at coyotes."

Dad glanced at Grandpa out of the corner of his eye. "Father," he said, "you don't fool me. You like this dog."

Grandpa Olsen didn't answer.

"You had Border collies for years," Dad said. "Some of them were wonderful dogs."

"Just a lot of trouble," Grandpa insisted.

Dad turned to me. "Get Grandpa to tell you about Scamp sometime. Now, that was a great dog!"

"Yes, Scamp was a good dog," Grandpa agreed suddenly. "A real cattle dog. Not like this one, I can tell you."

I hadn't realized that Grandpa had been watching us at the McGinness place.

"He can still be a good dog, even if he doesn't work cattle," I said, defending Jet.

"A dog is made to work," Grandpa said. "And if he can't work, he isn't worth anything."

I didn't answer. I had a sudden feeling that Grandpa was talking about more than dogs. I think he was talking about himself. I think he was thinking, *If a man can't work, he isn't worth anything.*

You're worth something to God, I thought. I wanted to say it out loud, but I was a big coward. For someone who talks so much I can have a hard time saying the right thing at the right time.

Dad shifted in his seat and sighed. "I was about your age when Grandpa first got Scamp, Mark. And even though I'm not a dog person, he was one dog that I really did like."

"He liked you kids, too," Grandpa said. "I never had to worry about *him* biting anyone." He glared at Jet for a moment, then turned to stare out the window again.

"Jet won't bite anyone," I said quickly.

Jet thumped his silky tail against the seat in agreement.

"Scamp liked me well enough," Dad continued. "Until Grandpa had cattle work to do. Then Scamp deserted me like a rat fleeing a sinking ship!"

"He was a working dog," Grandpa said, his voice a bit sharp.

"I know," Dad said. "But he didn't have to make it so obvious who he loved the most! If it was a contest between me and the cows, the cows won every time!"

I smiled to myself and rubbed the top of Jet's head. *You won't desert me for a bunch of dumb cows, will you?* I thought happily. *You'll love me the best.*

"The only thing that Scamp hated was water," Dad said. He looked at Grandpa with a grin, but Grandpa continued to stare stonily ahead.

"He didn't like water?" I asked.

Dad nodded.

"So what did he drink?"

Dad snorted. "No, Mark!" He rolled his eyes. "He didn't like to go in the water! And that was a problem since the Iron Creek runs right through the center of Grandpa's land."

"Scamp crossed the creek," Grandpa said.

Dad laughed. "Yeah, but he didn't like it. I can remember you yelling at him as he tried to tiptoe his way through the shallow spots. The cows would be miles ahead, and Scamp would still be gathering his courage to cross the creek!"

Grandpa's lips twitched as he remembered, but he didn't say anything.

It was quiet for a moment, and then Dad let out a chuckle. "I can remember one time Scamp crossed the creek faster than normal. It was the time your prize bull had foot rot. Remember, Dad?"

Grandpa shrugged his shoulders.

"You had this great big bull we called Sinbad," Dad went on. "And one day you found him limping in the pasture. He had an infection in one back foot and was terribly lame."

"I remember now," Grandpa said.

"Sinbad was on the other side of the creek," Dad said, glancing at me, "in a spot that Grandpa couldn't get to with the truck. We needed to chase the bull across the creek to a clear area so that Grandpa could take him home in the stock trailer."

Grandpa took up the story. "The water was really high that spring. I'd never have been able to drive the truck across, even at the main crossing."

Sinbad was so lame he'd hardly move, even when Scamp nipped at his heels," Dad said. "We were close to the creek but not at a place we normally crossed. Grandpa didn't want to make the bull walk any further, so he decided to try and chase him right across at that deep spot."

"What else could I do?" Grandpa growled. "You

know what happens when a critter gets foot rot. They can hardly walk."

Dad laughed. "You did the right thing, Dad, but it was a bit of a problem at the time. And Scamp got so frustrated trying to move the slow bull that he forgot how much he hated water."

"What happened?" I asked.

"The bull stopped right at the edge of the creek and planted his feet. He was determined that he wasn't going to move any more. And Scamp was just as determined that he was. That crazy dog jumped up, grabbed the bull by the end of his sensitive tail, and hung on. Sinbad let out an awful bellow and bolted straight across the creek!"

I laughed.

"Scamp refused to let go of the bull's tail, so old Sinbad towed him right across the creek like a water skier behind a motorboat!" Dad laughed. "I think it was the only time in Scamp's life that he crossed water as fast as a cow!"

Grandpa frowned. "Scamp was a good dog," he insisted.

"Jet's going to be a good dog, too," I said. I stroked the dog's silky coat, admiring his glossy hair. "And he's going to be really glad he came to live with us."

Jet leaned against my leg and began to hum. In a few moments the happy growl began to roll out of his throat again.

Dad looked at me and raised his eyebrows.

"It's nothing," I said quickly. "Mr. McGinness said Jet always growls when he's really happy."

"Really?"

"Really, Dad. Jet's not mad. He's a nice dog."

"He'll bite the baby," Grandpa said suddenly.

"What?" I asked.

"You better watch him around the baby," Grandpa said. "Border collies can be snappy."

I rolled my eyes but didn't say anything. Anyone could tell that Jet wasn't going to bite. Anyone except for my grandpa, that is, who was suddenly the world's expert on dogs.

4

Jet Meets the Family

Before long we pulled up in front of the hospital.

"Mark, I want you and Jet to stay in the truck," Dad ordered. "I'll help Grandpa to his room; then we'll head home."

"Are you going to be long?" I asked. A cow mooed loudly from the stock trailer behind us, as though it was asking the same thing.

"Nope," Dad assured me with a grin. "Don't want to keep the lassies waiting."

"Dad!"

"Don't I sound Scottish to you, ol' chap?"

Grandpa opened the truck door and swung his feet out. "Come on," he said. "This is why you're always late. Too much fooling around."

Jet jumped up as soon as the truck door opened. He darted through my legs, and in one quick bound stood at the open truck door.

I grabbed frantically for Jet's collar, but it slid

through my hands.

Jet hesitated at the open door, his eyes darting back and forth. I could almost hear him thinking, *Where am I? Where's the farm?*

I stretched as far as I could, but my seat belt kept me from reaching Jet's collar. "Here, Jet!" I called frantically. "Don't go outside!"

Jet's ears pricked forward, and his nose quivered. The stock trailer behind us rocked as the cows milled about, and Jet rocked, too. As I watched, the little dog crouched down, ready to spring out of the truck.

I was in a panic. What if Jet got away? He'd never even been off the McGinness farm before. He'd be lost immediately!

I fumbled with my seatbelt. "Jet!" I called again. "Stay!"

Jet sprang out of the truck. Well, he tried to spring out, but Grandpa was faster than Jet. He reached forward, and with a surprisingly strong hand caught Jet's collar.

"Get back, fool," Grandpa said sharply. He jerked Jet back into the truck.

Jet wagged his tail, then reached up and licked Grandpa Olsen on the cheek.

Grandpa pushed the collie away. "Crazy dog," he muttered. But at that moment I caught the first smile I had seen for a long time on Grandpa's face. Oh, it was a small smile, and brief, but it was a smile.

"Thanks for catching him, Grandpa." I sighed

with relief. I grabbed onto Jet's collar and pulled him close to me.

Grandpa didn't say anything, but his eyes seemed softer. He looked at me, and then at Jet, for a long moment. He turned back to the open truck door.

Dad came around to the other side of the truck with the wheelchair. "Quick thinking, Father," he said with a smile. Then Dad turned to me. "I'll be back in a few minutes," he said. He helped Grandpa slide into the wheelchair.

"Can Jet come in to visit?" I asked. "I could show him Grandpa's room."

Dad shook his head. "They don't allow dogs in the hospital," he said.

Jet stood on the truck floor, watching Dad and Grandpa. When they disappeared from sight, the dog shook himself and scrambled up onto the truck seat.

"Are you supposed to be up there?" I asked the dog. "That's Grandpa's spot."

Jet waved his tail back and forth.

"Well, at least you're more cheerful than the last person who sat there," I told the dog.

By now you probably think that I'm an awful person. What kind of kid says things like that about his own grandfather? Well, I want you to know that I'm trying to be a good person, a decent Christian kid—but sometimes it's hard.

I do love my Grandpa. After all, we go a long way back. Eleven years, to be exact. And Grandpa and I used to be so close. That's probably why I've found it really hard to be around him now that he's changed. I know how great he used to be, and I really don't appreciate the changes.

If my life were a TV show things would get better in about half an hour. My grandpa would cheer up, probably because of something wonderful I said or did, and I'd earn myself lots of new friends. But this isn't TV; it's real life. So I'm just struggling along, doing the best that I can. Which certainly doesn't seem good enough these days.

"Come on, you rascal," I told Jet, pulling him close to me. "Growl for me."

Jet smiled up at me and wiggled a bit closer.

Before long Dad was back at the hospital door. He stopped for a moment and began to talk to a teenage boy I didn't recognize. The boy was leading a handsome golden retriever, and they were heading into the hospital. Dad rubbed the dog's head and pointed toward us, then waved goodbye before starting toward our truck.

Jet, who had been standing proudly on the truck seat, suddenly pricked his ears forward. He looked at Dad, then bounced off the seat and scooted back onto the floor.

I glanced at Jet suspiciously. "What're you doing?" I asked the dog. "Trying to stay out of trouble?"

Jet sighed and rested his chin on the truck seat. He looked at me with innocent eyes and waved his tail back and forth.

I smiled. There was nothing wrong with this dog's thinking!

"All right," Dad said, opening the truck door. "We're off."

"Who was that?" I asked.

"Who?"

"That guy you were talking to," I said. "Who was it?"

"That's Stephen Klinger," Dad said. "One of our neighbors."

"He had *his* dog at the hospital," I said.

"I didn't see a dog," Dad said. His eyes twinkled.

"Dad!" I groaned. "You bent over and scratched the dog."

"I doubt it," Dad said. "I don't like dogs."

"Dad!" I groaned. "You're pulling my leg."

Dad's eyes opened wide, and he looked down at my legs. "I never touched you," he said firmly. "Now did I, ol' chap?"

I laughed, and Jet's eyes sparkled. He wagged his tail as though he enjoyed the joke, too.

"Why did he have his dog at the hospital?" I asked. "I thought hospitals didn't allow dogs."

Dad nodded his head. "I was surprised, too," he said. "But he says that the hospital has a pet therapy program."

"You scratched the dog," I stated.

Dad tightened his lips, and then nodded his head.

"Do you really hate dogs?" I asked.

"Oh, I do!" Dad insisted. "I hate dogs a lot."

"Grandpa doesn't," I said thoughtfully. "I wonder if he'd like Jet to visit him at the hospital someday."

"I don't know what he'd think about that," Dad said.

"He likes Jet," I said. "I saw him smile when Jet licked his face. Maybe that's what Grandpa needs— someone who likes him, even when he's a grouch."

Dad smiled. "Son," he said. "I think that's a wonderful idea. Maybe you can help him. I've just about given up."

Mom met us at the door of the entryway. She looked tired. Her hair was messy, and I could hear Baby Ryan crying in the background.

"You're late," she said. "I think supper's burned. You should have phoned me, Rob." She paced around the entryway, picking up scattered boots and mittens while talking.

"Sorry," Dad said. He stomped the snow off his boots.

"Guess what, Mom?" I said, still standing outside.

"Were you born in a barn, Mark?" she said crossly. "Come inside and shut the door. It's freezing out there."

"Just a minute," I said, tugging on Jet's leash.

"What stinks?" Mom asked. She wrinkled her nose. "Is it your boots? I bet you men stepped in a pile of cow manure!"

"It's not our boots," I said, stepping into the entryway. "It's Jet."

Jet slunk out of the shadows behind me and peered nervously through the open door. He wagged his tail hesitantly when he saw Mom. He wanted to be friendly, but he was frightened. I don't think Jet had actually realized that there was a world out there besides the McGinness's yard.

"A dog!" Mom shrieked.

I watched her face anxiously. Mom didn't seem to know what to think. An uncertain smile flickered on her face, and then she wrinkled her forehead.

"A dog?" she asked. "Whose dog is this?"

"He's mine," I said. I had to pull on the leash to coax Jet into the house. He crept in nervously and sat down close to me.

"What do you mean, Mark?" Mom asked. She turned to look at Dad. "Robert Olsen, why didn't you tell me that you were getting a dog?"

Dad shrugged his shoulders sheepishly. "I didn't know I was," he said.

Mom stared at him, then slowly bent over. She scratched Jet under the chin. Jet began to wag his tail, slowly at first, and then faster and faster. Soon his whole rear end was wagging back and forth. Her smile grew a bit bigger. "Well," she said. "At least it's a nice dog."

"Dad says you hate dogs," I said. "Do you?"

Mom laughed. "I've always wanted a dog," she said. She thought for a moment, and her smile slowly faded away. "But Mark, I honestly don't have any time for a pet right now."

"I'll take care of Jet, Mom," I pleaded. "Honest."

"What's he going to be like with the baby?" Mom asked.

"I'll keep him away from Ryan," I said.

Mom sighed and ran her fingers through her hair. "OK," she said finally. "We'll give it a try. But come on, guys. You need to eat supper."

"Is it worth eating?" Dad asked.

Mom made a swipe at Dad's backside. "Listen, fella," she said, "no complaining! If you'd have been home on time it would have been perfect."

I looked at Jet. He was sitting as close to me as possible, his head pressed against my leg. I think touching me made him feel a bit safer.

"Put him outside," Dad said. "He's making the entryway stink."

"He can't sleep outside," Mom said. "It's too cold."

"He's an outdoor dog," Dad said. "Look at his thick hair."

"Yes," Mom agreed. "But he needs a warm dog-house to sleep in."

"Mr. Fix-it here says he'll build one tomorrow, but I'm not holding my breath," Daid said.

"You wait and see, Dad," I said. "I can build a super house."

"Ha!" Dad snorted. "Out of a cardboard box, maybe."

Mom glanced around the entryway. "Speaking of cardboard boxes, maybe I have something packed that Jet can sleep on." Her eyes came to rest on a big box in the corner of the room. She rummaged in it and came up with a tattered pillow.

"Here," Mom said. "I wondered why I kept this ratty thing."

"We don't even know if he's housebroken," Dad said.

"I guess we'll find out," Mom answered with a sigh. She cleared a place for the pillow, then called to the little dog. "Here you go, Jet," she said. "A place for you to sleep."

Jet seemed to understand her. He crept over to the pillow and lay down quickly. He put his nose between his paws and closed his eyes.

"Jet's a Christian dog," I said, looking at the Border collie.

"A Christian dog?" Dad asked.

"Look—he's praying," I said. "See how he has his paws folded and his eyes closed?"

"He's probably praying that he can sleep outside in the nice fresh air," Dad said.

"He's probably praying that you men will quit bugging him and let him get some rest," Mom said.

"I think he's thanking God for me," I said quickly. "He knows that I'm going to be the perfect dog owner."

Things were finally looking up for the Marvelous Mark and his "no-good" dog!

5

A Trip to the Bathtub

My new school is very small. Teeny tiny, actually. We have 12 kids (including me) and one teacher, who's just about as frazzled as my mom. Mrs. Weber is a very nice lady, but she's kept busy with all of our different grades. You couldn't pay me enough money to teach church school. I think I'd rather chase cows. At least cows will only run over and trample you. Kids can be worse.

My old public school had 300 kids. There were 28 in my class. Now I am the only student in grade five. The only boys who are close to me in age are Graham Stout and Chad Peterson, who are both in grade six.

You might think that Graham would be fat, his last name being Stout and all, but he isn't. He's tall and strong and lives on a farm only a few miles away from me. Chad is shorter and heavier, and lives somewhere south of us. He hasn't been very friendly. Chad doesn't even look at me when I try to talk to him.

Maybe he thinks I'll go away if he doesn't notice me.

Graham and Chad have been best friends since grade one, and they don't seem to be very interested in new kids. They have each other, after all.

Today was different, though. As soon as I got to school I told everyone about my new dog. I probably talked too much, but the kids were listening for once, and I wasn't about to miss my opportunity.

"I love dogs," Graham told me at recess. "My family has a Border collie too. Where did you get yours?"

"From Mr. McGinness," I said.

"Old Man McGinness!" Graham exclaimed. "He's got some great Border collies! I bet you paid a lot of money for your dog!"

"Not really," I hedged.

"Of course you did," Graham insisted. "My dad says that Old Man McGinness can get almost a thousand bucks for a well-trained cow dog. Even his puppies are expensive."

"I guess he gave us a good deal," I said. I wasn't about to tell Graham that Jet was a cull.

"He's a fool dog," Mr. McGinness had said, "and he'll never be worth anything."

Well, Jet was already worth something to me, and having Graham Stout talk to me like I was a real, honest-to-goodness person was worth something, too. I wasn't about to blow it by detailing all Jet's faults.

"He's a terrific dog," I said. "Wait until you see all the tricks I'm teaching him."

"What kinds of tricks?" Graham asked.

Chad had been standing a few feet away, wearing a bored expression. Now he began to shuffle his feet on the sidewalk. "Come on, Graham," he said impatiently. "The snow's perfect for a snowball fight, and you're wasting our time."

"Just a minute!" Graham said. He looked back at me. "What kinds of tricks are you working on?"

"I'm going to teach him everything," I said eagerly. "I'll start with the easy tricks first, of course. You know—sit, stay, down."

Graham nodded his head. "My dog can do those."

"Then I'll teach Jet to shake a paw and roll over and play dead," I continued.

"Uh-huh," Graham said.

"And then he can learn to jump through a hoop," I went on. "I saw that on TV once—lions jumping through flaming hoops. Of course, Jet's not a lion, but it's the same principle, I think. Hey! I wonder how they make the hoop burn without burning up? Sort of like Moses and the burning bush, right?"

Graham looked a little confused but nodded his head.

"Anyhow, I won't start with fire," I said. "Plain hoops will be enough. My parents would probably kill me if I did something dangerous like using burning hoops."

Chad groaned, but I didn't pause long enough to let him get a word in edgewise.

"And I thought I'd teach Jet to stand on his back

feet and dance. I once saw a poodle that could push a baby carriage. He stood on his back feet and pushed the carriage with his front feet. It was really cool, and I'm sure Jet can do anything a poodle can do."

I knew I was babbling but couldn't seem to stop.

"Well . . ." Graham sounded doubtful.

"I don't have a baby carriage," I said quickly, "but my little brother has a stroller, and that's almost the same thing, isn't it? Jet could push the stroller. Maybe he could even push my baby brother in the stroller!"

Graham laughed.

"That's perfect!" I said. "Jet could push Ryan outside so we all could get some peace and quiet in the house. You'd have to see my brother to know what that means. He's horrible; screams all the time. It drives me crazy, you know. But Jet could be a real help—kind of like a doggy babysitter or something."

Graham laughed again. "You have some pretty wild ideas," he said.

"Jet's really smart," I said. "He can do almost anything."

"Except talk," Graham said with a grin.

"The stupid dog doesn't need to talk," Chad growled. "His owner talks enough for them both."

I laughed.

"You'll have to show me this wonderful dog," Graham said as the school bell rang. "Maybe I can come over to your place someday."

"You want to come over to *my* house?" I asked. I

had to stop myself from looking around the school-yard to see if Graham was talking to someone else.

"Yeah," Graham said. "I'd like to see your dog."

"Sure," I said. "I'll try to fit that in my busy schedule!"

Graham looked puzzled for a moment. I guess he didn't know if I was joking or not.

"Just kidding," I said quickly. "I've got lots of time; come over, any day at all. That would be great."

Chad picked up a handful of snow and squeezed it tightly. "You can't go over tomorrow," he said, making the snow into a ball. "You're coming over to my place. Remember?"

"I remember," Graham said. "But maybe I'll come over another day."

"Yeah, sure," Chad said. "Whatever."

Mrs. Weber knocked on the school window, beckoning for us. Chad frowned at me and threw the snowball down on the sidewalk before hurrying into school. I had a suspicion that he would have rather thrown the snowball at me. But he didn't, so at least that was a step in the right direction.

The first thing I did when I got home from school was call for Jet. He came running across the yard, his ears flapping and his tail wagging.

"Did you miss me, Jet?" I asked, giving the dog a pat on the shoulder.

Jet smiled up at me, his whole body wagging with happiness.

"We've got a little problem with your dog," Mom

called from the deck of the house.

"What's wrong with Jet?" I asked anxiously.

"He scares me a little," Mom said. "At first I thought he was a nice dog, but when I was petting him this afternoon, he growled at me."

"He didn't mean anything by it," I said quickly. "Jet always growls when he's happy."

"Don't tell me stories, Mark," Mom warned. "Dogs don't growl when they're happy."

"Jet does," I said.

"Come on!"

"No, really," I said. That's what Mr. McGinness said. And he said that Jet's mom growls when she's happy, too."

"You should have told me that," Mom said. "He had me kinda worried there. Especially when Ryan kept wanting to pet him."

"Keep that kid away from my dog," I said quickly.

"Don't worry; Jet's been outside most of the day," Mom said. "Chasing birds."

She pointed to the lilac bush that stood besides the house. At first I didn't see anything, but when I looked carefully I saw a fresh path around the bush.

"The sparrows live in that bush," Mom said. "And he spent all day chasing them out of it, and then following them around the yard."

As if on cue, a flock of brown sparrows fluttered across the yard and into the lilac bush. Jet's ears suddenly pricked up and his tail rose stiffly above his back. With a sudden leap Jet bounded forward. He raced across the yard toward the shrubs. When he was near, he jumped into the air as though he was on springs, almost bouncing into the bush.

A cloud of sparrows shot out of the shrubs and swirled angrily across the yard. Jet was right behind them, running as fast as he could. Once he sprang into the air, soaring almost three feet high before landing on the run.

"Now I know why they called him Jet," Mom said. "He thinks he can fly."

I guess Mr. McGinness was right, I told myself. *Jet's not a cow dog, he's a bird dog!*

"He needs a bath," Mom reminded me. "Why don't you do it now?"

I called Jet into the entryway. This time he didn't hesitate at the doorway but trotted straight into the house and flopped down on his pillow.

"We did have one exciting moment this morning," Mom said, scratching Jet behind the ears. "Thanks to your little brother."

"What did Ryan do?" I asked with a frown.

My little brother, Ryan, had his first birthday a few weeks ago. He's not old enough to be a real boy yet, but you couldn't call him a baby, either. However, you *could* call him a brat. He got into my bedroom recently and pulled all the books off my bookshelf. He ripped a poster off my wall, dropped—and bent—my one and only hockey trophy, and drew on the linoleum with some felt pens.

I wanted Mom to spank him, but she just sighed and took him out of my room. I had to scrub the floor with cleaner, and I had to put all the books back. The poster was ruined, and no one bought me a new one. Now you know why I had a sinking feeling when I heard that Ryan had been bothering Jet.

"What did Ryan do this time?" I growled.

Mom sighed. She sighs a lot lately, especially since we moved. "He sat on Jet," she said. "Hard."

"Sat on Jet!" I exclaimed. "How? Why?"

"Jet was sound asleep in the entryway this morning," Mom said. "Maybe he was even dreaming, I don't know, but his tail and paws were twitching. Ryan walked into the room and stood there staring at Jet. I thought he was just looking. That's what he had been doing all morning, running into the entryway and looking at Jet. Then he'd scream, and run back into the kitchen."

I could imagine the noise. Ryan likes to yell. He yells when he's happy, and he yells when he's mad. Ryan's noisy every waking minute of the day. That's just the way he is. Dad said that I had been like that, too. (I guess the Marvelous Mark and the Mighty Moving Mouth had to have a start somewhere.) But two noisy kids in our house is one too many. If you know what I mean.

"Anyhow," Mom continued, "I thought he was just going to look at Jet when all of a sudden I heard a thump. Ryan had turned around and sat down on top of the poor dog."

"Ryan!"

"He sat down hard, too," Mom said. "Knocked the wind out of poor old Jet here." She patted the dog softly. "Jet shot straight up in the air. I didn't even see him get his legs under him; he just bounced straight up like a rubber ball. His eyes were as wide as saucers."

"What did he do next?"

"I was terrified that he would bite," Mom said. "After all, he had growled at me earlier that morning, so I didn't know what to expect. But he was really good. He jumped backward when he lit, and then just stood there staring at Ryan."

"Maybe he *should* bite Ryan," I said sourly. "That would teach him to keep away from Jet."

"No!" Mom exclaimed. "He shouldn't! We couldn't keep a dog that bites, even if Ryan did start it. And Jet seemed to know that he shouldn't hurt the baby. He shut his mouth, and then stomped over to the door and asked to be let outside. That's where he's stayed for the rest of the day."

"Good boy!" I praised the dog. I spent several minutes scratching him all over. If I paused for a moment, Jet would nudge me with his nose, reminding me to keep scratching. I'm sure Jet didn't know why I was so happy, but he enjoyed the attention without asking any questions. Before long he was humming his happy growl, his eyes tightly closed, and his tail wagging wildly.

"Now, if that dog is going to continue to sleep in the house, he needs a bath," Mom said. "Why don't you run the water in the tub, and I'll find an old towel to dry him with."

I filled the bathtub half-full of warm water, then called Jet. He left the entry way hesitantly and followed me closely down the narrow hallway to the bathroom. When Jet saw the tub full of water, his ears went down and his tail tucked between his legs. He refused to enter the bathroom, so I finally had to pick him up and carry him through the door.

"What's the matter with you?" I puffed, kicking the door partially closed behind us. "Don't tell me you're scared of the water!"

I scratched the dog's head reassuringly. "Maybe all Border collies are scared of water," I laughed. "Come on, sissy!" I grabbed Jet in my arms and lifted him over the edge of the tub.

Jet raised his legs as I lowered him toward the water. The closer he got to the water, the higher his legs went. He tried to clamber out of my arms, and I had to hold him tightly. Finally he stood in the tub, one front leg still raised out of the water, and whimpered.

"Don't be such a chicken," I told the dog. "A bath isn't going to hurt you."

Jet cried again, a loud, sad wail, and tried to climb out of the tub.

"Stay!" I ordered loudly. I scooped up a bucket of warm water and carefully poured it down the dog's back. Moving slowly, I wet Jet down from front to back, then leaned forward to reach for the shampoo. I had turned away from Jet for only a second, but he saw his opportunity.

Jet bounded over the edge of the tub and landed on the floor with a wet *smack.* Droplets of water flew everywhere.

"Jet!" I yelled. "Get back here, you big coward!"

Jet paused at the door of the bathroom and shot me a desperate look. I lunged at the dog, but he slipped through my hands like a greased pig and galloped around the corner.

"Oh, no!" I moaned.

I spun around to race after Jet, but one of my sock feet hit a puddle of water. My foot slid out from under me, and I fell backward with a crash. The back of my head hit the tub. I actually saw stars, and a flare of white-hot pain made my eyes water. It wasn't tears, of course, but it was the next thing to it. Hey, it hurt!

I lay on the bathroom floor for a moment, trying to get my bearings.

A sudden loud Ryan scream came from down the hallway.

I groaned and scrambled back to my feet. With one hand on my head, I stumbled toward the sound of the yelling. I was almost there when Jet shot past me again. He was running flat out and whizzed past me, leaving a shower of water drops on the hall wall.

"That crazy dog just came in here and shook!"

Mom yelled. "He's soaked the whole place."

Ryan screamed again, louder than ever.

Dad picked that moment to walk into the house. I came around the entryway corner just in time to see Jet crash full force into Dad.

Dad staggered backward into the clothes closet. He grabbed for something to keep him upright. I saw the closet pole bend under Dad's weight, and then there was a sharp crack! The closet pole broke in two. Dad and the entire load of coats, snowsuits, overalls, and winter pants fell in a heap at the bottom of the closet.

Jet seemed to know he was in trouble. He dove for the entryway door, hoping to get out, but it was tightly closed. He hit the door with a thump and crouched at the doorway, his tail wagging feebly. I knew he was trying to say, "Whoops! Sorry! Just an accident."

Dad groaned loudly from the closet floor. A broom at the back of the closet took that moment to tip forward and crack him on his forehead before hitting the floor.

Dad let out another moan.

Jet squirmed over to the pile of boots and tried to hide behind them.

Ryan toddled to the entryway door and stared at the scene in front of him. His clothes were soaked with water, and his eyes were big and round. He looked at Jet, and then at Dad, who was still lying in the heap of clothing in the closet. Ryan's lips trembled. I didn't know whether he was going to cry or laugh.

Finally, Dad propped himself up on one elbow. "What hit me?" he groaned again. "Did anyone get the name of that truck?"

Jet crept across the entryway floor, his belly never leaving the floor. He slithered right up to Dad and buried his wet head under Dad's arm, trying to hide.

"You!" Dad said, glaring at the little dog.

"He didn't mean to, Daddy," I said. I rubbed the goose egg on the back of my head and quickly trotted into the entryway. I pulled Jet away from Dad. The dog's tail wagged feebly, and he rolled over so I could rub his belly.

"Poor Jet," I said soothingly. "I guess you don't like baths."

"Poor Jet!" Dad sputtered. "What about poor Dad?"

Ryan began to scream. Mom hurried around the corner and picked up the little boy. Then she stopped and stared at Dad. "Robert!" she gasped. "What are you doing?"

"Just having a little nap, dear," Dad drawled.

"In the closet?"

"I was tired."

The corners of Mom's lips began to twitch. Suddenly she burst into loud laughter. She laughed so hard that tears began to run down her cheeks, and she finally had to sit down on the hallway floor with Ryan still tucked in her arms.

"What's so funny?" Dad growled. But a faint smile

began to spread across his face, too.

Mom couldn't answer. She laughed and waved her hands and wiped tears away from her eyes. Then she laughed some more.

Ryan stopped yelling and stared at Mom in amazement.

Mom finally straightened up. She took one last look at Dad, who was now sitting in the heap of clothing, and then she blew her nose.

"Thanks," she said. "I needed that!"

Dad glared at me one last time before struggling to his feet. "I didn't need that," he muttered. "Get busy, Mark. You have a dog house to build!"

6

Jet
Visits Grandpa

It was Sabbath afternoon. Mom and Dad and baby Ryan were dressed in their best clothes, ready to go to the hospital with other people from our church to sing to the patients. For the past half hour Mom had been twisting my arm, trying to persuade me to come with them. I didn't want to go. Nobody my age would be there, and I had no interest in singing. But my mom can be pretty "persuasive."

"Get dressed," she finally said, frowning. "You're coming with us."

"You know I can't sing," I pointed out.

"There's nothing wrong with your singing," Mom argued.

"Right," I groaned, rolling my eyes. "Remember last year's Christmas concert? Miss Blume was furious at me because she thought I was singing awful on purpose."

Mom smiled faintly and nodded her head.

"I was singing the best I could," I said. "Honestly. I just naturally sound horrible."

"I didn't think you were that bad," Dad said. "Especially when I had my fingers in my ears."

"Very funny, Dad."

Dad slipped a tie around his neck and began to snug it into place. "If I ever find the person who invented ties," he muttered, "I'll put something around his neck and tighten it up. Real tight."

"Here, let me do it," Mom offered. She flipped the end of the tie around and began to do up the knot.

"I'm going outside," I told my parents casually. "Maybe I'll check on the cows."

"Since when have you been interested in cows?" Dad asked.

"Only recently," I answered.

"Tomorrow you'd better show a bit of interest in doghouses," Dad continued. "Remember our deal? You were going to make one for Jet."

"I could start today," I said quickly.

"Good try, Mark," Dad said, "but it's not going to work. Go put on your church clothes—we're leaving in a few minutes."

"I can't sing," I insisted.

"That's it!" Mom said. "I'm going to enroll you in piano lessons. Then you'll have a musical talent."

"Mom!" I said. "I'm not musical. And I don't want to learn to play the piano."

"How about the tuba?" Dad teased.

"Or the tuba," I said. "Or anything. I don't like music."

"You still need to come with us," Mom said. "It's a good way to use your talents for God."

I sighed. "Face it, Mom," I said. "I don't have a single musical talent in my body. In fact, I don't think I have any special talents at all."

"You're wrong about that," Dad said. "God gives everyone gifts and talents."

"Not me," I said.

"Yes, even you," Dad insisted. "God gives every single person talents to use to serve Him and others. Some people sing or play a musical instrument to serve Him. Others serve Him with their teaching abilities. Or their art."

"I rest my case," I said. "I can't teach, and I'm not an artist. God just overlooked me when He was handing out talents!"

Dad laughed.

"Of course, He made up for it by giving me an extra helping of good looks and charm," I said. "So I guess I'll manage without talents."

Mom rolled her eyes. "Mark, you're a nut," she said. "And maybe that's one of the gifts God gave you."

"Being a nut?" I asked.

"Our personality traits can be used to serve God," Mom continued. "Or they can be used to serve Satan. You can use your humor to help others, or to put them down, right?"

"You want me to tell jokes at the hospital?" I asked. "Like a stand-up comedian?"

"No," Mom sighed. "Just be yourself. Cheer up people."

"Use your gift of gab wisely," Dad said. "That's one of the talents that God gave you."

"I wonder where he got that from?" Mom asked.

"What? His gift of gab?" Dad shrugged. "I have no idea."

"So let me get this straight," I said. "You want me to come to the hospital and stand around talking to a bunch of people who I've never met before?"

"Sure. Why not?"

"I can't do that," I groaned. "Who wants to listen to a dumb kid?"

Dad glared at me. "Enough," he said. "Get dressed in some good clothes. We're going in a few minutes. You can visit with Grandpa if you don't want to sing. I'm sure he'd love to see you."

"I'm sure he wouldn't," I said. "He doesn't like anything these days."

Then a thought hit me like a bolt of lightning. I knew someone—or should I say something—that Grandpa would probably like to see. Something that would interest him more than church music.

"Can I bring Jet?" I asked.

Mom shook her head.

"The hospital lets people bring their dogs," I insisted. "Remember, Dad? And I know that Grandpa likes Jet. I can visit him in his room while you guys are singing."

Mom shook her head again, but Dad put his hand up. "You may have a point there," he said. "I'm pretty sure Grandpa won't be down for the music. Maybe he would like to see Jet."

And that's how Jet and I ended up in the backseat of the car with Ryan beside us, screaming blue murder. I told you that Ryan yells a lot. He especially hates his car seat, which makes traveling with him a real pain. A pain in the neck, and a pain in the ears.

Jet ignored Ryan and stared out the car window. He looked especially handsome. Mom and I had managed to finish his bath, and his black hair shone with an iridescent hue. His white ruff and paws were as clean as the new fallen snow, and he was wearing a bright red collar that I had bought in town at the drugstore.

"Try to be a good dog," I told Jet, scratching him under his chin. He waved his tail slowly. *I'm always a good dog,* he seemed to say.

We ran into our first problem at the hospital door.

Jet took one look, or should I say one listen, to the hiss of the sliding glass door, and he backed up with his tail tucked between his legs.

"It's not a rattlesnake," I said, shaking my head. "And it's not going to hurt you."

Jet wasn't convinced. He stood at the end of his leash, as far away from the sliding doors as he could possibly get, and planted his feet. He wasn't about to move.

"Show him how it works," Mom suggested.

I passed her Jet's leash and walked up to the hospital door. They slid open, and I walked inside the hospital. Then I turned around and walked out again.

"See, chicken," I said, "that didn't hurt me, did it?"

Jet wagged his tail weakly and backed up a few steps farther.

"I thought Border collies were supposed to be so smart," I told Jet. "At least that's what my dog book said. 'Border collies: the smartest breed of them all.'"

"Maybe Jet didn't read the book," Dad said. He sighed and bent down, picked up Jet, and hauled him ungracefully through the doors and into the hospital.

"Thanks, Dad," I said.

Dad frowned and plucked several white dog hairs off the front of his suit jacket.

Once we were inside Jet saw something wonderful, something that made his whole body quiver with excitement. *People!* Everywhere he looked were nice people who had nothing better to do than pet him! It took me five minutes just to get through the front of the hospital. Office staff and nurses and sick people of all sizes and shapes wanted to pet Jet, and he was happy to oblige. When someone petted him, he wagged his tail so hard his whole body shook.

When the Sunshine Band started singing, Jet and I stood for a minute to listen. Then I slipped away and headed down the long hallway to Grandpa's room. His door was half open. I knocked on the door and waited.

When there was no answer, I knocked again, then pushed on the door. "Grandpa?" I called.

"I told you to go away," a voice growled.

I hesitated. Was that Grandpa? Was he talking to me?

The rest of the hospital was cheery and bright, but Grandpa's room was dim. It kind of gave me the creeps. You know, the perfect room out of a horror movie—dark and gloomy. All we needed was a bit of thunder and lightning in the background to complete the mood.

I stood with one foot in Grandpa's room and one foot out in the hallway. Should I go in? I'm much too old to be scared of the dark and such, but somehow I couldn't make my feet move into the room. *I should respect my elders,* I thought quickly. *Is it fair for me to force myself upon Grandpa if he doesn't want to see me? I think I'll just go away, and find something else to do.*

Yes, that sounded like a fine idea. I'd just swing the door shut and sneak away. No one would even need to know I had been there. Grandpa certainly didn't care. Just what kind of Grandpa was he, anyway? If he didn't love me anymore, then I certainly wasn't going to bother with him.

Jet didn't seem to be on the same track as I was. While I stood in the doorway, being pulled one way and then the other by my own worries and concerns, Jet made up his mind. He smelled Grandpa inside the room and must have decided that the nice man that he'd met in the truck the other day was longing to scratch a poor Border collie's head again!

And when it was apparent that I didn't know what to do, Jet took things into his own hands—or should I say, his own paws. Jet bounded forward, slipping through the narrow open crack in the door so quickly that I was taken by surprise. The leash slid through my fingers, and then Jet was gone.

"Hey!" A shout from inside the room was followed by a loud thump.

I quickly pushed the door open and stepped into Grandpa's room. The curtains were pulled tightly shut, leaving the room dull and gloomy. In the dim light I could make out Grandpa, sitting in his wheelchair. Jet had his long black nose buried in Grandpa's lap, and Grandpa was petting the top of his head.

"Hi, Grandpa," I called, "It's me, Mark."

"Well, I didn't think it was the Avon lady," Grandpa said. "Come on in."

His invitation surprised me a bit. "May I turn on the light?" I asked.

"I guess so," Grandpa said.

I fumbled around by the door until I found the switch. The room lit up with a blinding glare. Grandpa looked at me and blinked. He had a faint smile on his face, and his frosty blue eyes had a hint of a twinkle in them.

"Your dog scared me half to death," Grandpa said. "He poked his cold nose right between my shirt buttons! Just about made me jump out of the lousy wheelchair."

I didn't know if I was supposed to laugh, or apologize, so I didn't say anything.

"I guess it could have been worse," Grandpa went on. "For a moment there I thought one of them young nurses were getting fresh or something!"

Now I did laugh.

"What's so funny?" Grandpa asked. "Do you think I'm too old for them nurses? Well, I ain't!"

I laughed again. "I'm just surprised," I said. "I haven't seen you cheerful for a long time."

Then I flushed beet-red. That sounded awful. Isn't that just like me to open my mouth and let the words come tumbling out without thinking about what I was saying!

Grandpa gave a little cackle of a laugh. His voice was hoarse, as if he wasn't used to laughing anymore.

"OK," he said, "so I've been a bit crabby lately, have I?"

"You could say that."

Grandpa rubbed Jet's ears thoughtfully. "Well," he finally said, "I've had plenty of reasons to be upset, wouldn't you agree?"

I shrugged. "I guess so."

Jet gave Grandpa's hand a lick and pressed closer to the wheelchair. "So how's this worthless dog doing?" Grandpa asked. "I imagine that you're outside most days trying to make him chase your cows, aren't you?"

"Why do you think that?" I asked.

"Because you're a boy," Grandpa said. "And all boys want to push big things around. Some push cows, and others push their dads."

"I have tried once or twice," I admitted. "But Jet won't chase them. Oh, he'll stand on the outside of the corral and bark at the cows, but as soon as they turn to face him, he runs away. He's a bit of a chicken, you know."

"A chicken?" Grandpa asked.

I nodded my head. "He's scared of a lot of things."

"Like what?"

I thought for a moment. "Cows, for one thing," I said. "And baths. And doors."

"Doors?"

"Well, he sure doesn't like the hospital's sliding doors," I said. "Dad had to carry him inside, and he got hair on his good suit. I don't think he was very happy about it, either."

"Who wasn't happy?" Grandpa asked. "Your dad or Jet?"

I snickered. "Neither of them were very impressed with the whole deal," I said.

"Well, I don't suppose ol' McGinness would have given him to you if he thought he'd ever be a cattle dog," Grandpa said. "Mr. McGinness is known for getting his money out of things. They say he can stretch a penny so far it's nothing more than a copper wire when he's done with it."

"He's cheap, you mean?"

"Frugal," Grandpa said. "Scotch, but not cheap. Ol' McGinness will spend plenty of money on things he wants, but he doesn't intend to waste it on foolishness."

"Is he your friend?" I asked.

"McGinness?" Grandpa snorted. Then he thought for a moment. "Well, I suppose so."

"Then why didn't you talk to him last week when we picked up the cows?"

Grandpa's face grew suddenly cold. "What do you mean?" he asked.

I hesitated, but Grandpa glared at me, daring me to say something. And you know Marvelous Mark—I just can't keep my mouth closed for long.

"I don't get it," I said. "You say that Mr. McGinness is your friend, but you wouldn't talk to him when we were at his farm. You didn't even look at him."

"Do you think I *want* him to talk to me?" Grandpa practically shouted. "And look at me? Never!"

"Why not?" I asked, honestly confused.

"Why not?" Grandpa looked down at his legs. "I don't want anyone to see me like this, stuck in this chair! It makes for great talk down at the local coffee shop, I suppose: 'Poor old Olsen, stuck like a big baby in his wheelchair, with a bunch of nurses young enough to be his grandkids taking care of him!'"

"But that's what nurses are supposed to do," I said. "If no one was sick, nurses wouldn't have jobs, now would they?"

Grandpa's face flushed red. The room was deadly

quiet for a minute. I could hear music in the distance, and someone in the hallway laughed. But the only sound in Grandpa's room was the soft ticking of the clock that hung over his bed.

Jet stood quietly by Grandpa, but when the man didn't move, he finally got impatient and pushed his nose into Grandpa's hand again, looking for attention.

"Come here, boy," I called to the dog.

Jet looked at me and wagged his tail. Then he pushed his head against Grandpa again.

Grandpa sighed and looked down at the dog.

"He's been a good dog," I said, getting up from the bed and stroking Jet's long hair.

"Hmmph," Grandpa grunted. "I'll bet the fool dog's been chasing birds, hasn't he?"

This is absolutely amazing, I thought. This was the closest to being cheerful that Grandpa had looked since his stroke.

I nodded. "He's worn paths all around the bushes," I explained. "He runs nonstop."

"I figured so," Grandpa said. His hands were gentle on Jet's head. "Border collies are fools for running."

"He's a good dog," I said again.

"Some idiots get a Border collie when they live in the city," Grandpa said. "It makes the poor dogs miserable. A collie can't live if he doesn't run. If it isn't after cows, it's after birds or kids or something else. He's got to be busy."

Grandpa's face twisted down. He suddenly quit

talking and looked down at his wheelchair. "I guess I'm like that, too," Grandpa said softly. "I can't stand thinkin' that I'll never be able to run or work again. What kind of life is that for a man?"

I didn't know what to say. Yeah, I can be a bit of a know-it-all, but I really don't know everything. Adults were supposed to help *me* with *my* problems. How could I help them with theirs?

I had a sudden thought, though. God had all the answers. I prayed a quick prayer, asking God to give me the wisdom to say something smart. Something so profound and brilliant that it would help Grandpa see that his life wasn't over. Something so he could see that God loved him, and that we did, too.

I guess God didn't have time to answer my prayer that day, because I can honestly say I didn't get any inspiration. I couldn't think of anything wise or helpful to say.

I mean, Grandpa did have a problem. It wasn't something that could be solved very easily.

And I didn't know what to say. So I sat in the room and watched while Grandpa petted Jet. We didn't say much, but at least Grandpa wasn't yelling at me, and that was something.

But I could have done better. If only God would have given me the right answer at the right time. But it never happened, and that's all there was to it.

7

Friends at Long Last

First, the good news. On Monday, after school, Graham Stout came over to my house. Now the bad news. Chad Peterson came, too.

I think Chad only came to keep an eye on Graham. You know, to make sure that we didn't get too friendly. Chad wasn't about to risk losing his best friend to a geeky grade five kid like me.

It was the first day in February, and the weather was finally decent. Snow was melting off the roof of our house, making puddles on our deck. Jet was delighted to see the boys. He galloped over to Graham, who gave him a big scratch, then raced over to Chad.

Chad wasn't too thrilled to see Jet. "Get lost, dog," he said. He raised his foot and pushed Jet away.

Jet wasn't about to let a little foot stand in the way of a good friendship. He pushed past Chad's leg and pressed his head cheerfully against Chad. He began his soft happy growl deep in his throat, his tail moving back and forth.

"Scram!" Chad said. He backed up a step and glared at Jet.

Jet must have thought Chad was being playful, because he trotted across the yard and picked up a stick and brought it back to Chad. Jet dropped the stick by Chad's feet and barked.

"He wants you to throw the stick," I told Chad.

"I don't like dogs," Chad said, "and I'm not throwing him that stupid stick."

"I'll throw it," Graham said. He reached over and grabbed the branch. "Here, Jet. Go get it." Graham reared back and threw the stick with all his might across the yard.

Jet barked happily and tore after the stick. Now this was fun! Three terrific boys to play with, and the perfect fetching stick!

After a few minutes Chad began to get restless. "I'm freezing," he complained.

"It's nice out," Graham said, with a grin. He grabbed the stick from Jet's mouth and threw it again. "And I'm having fun."

There was a loud bawl from the corral from one of the cows. They were always hungry. "Eating for two," Dad had explained.

"Hey, let's go see your cows," Graham said.

"They're just your regular type cows," I told him. "You know, four legs and a head."

"I like animals," Graham said. "And I'd like to see them."

That solved that. "OK," I agreed, starting forward. Right about now I'd have tried to help Graham fly to the moon if he'd asked. I'd have done just about anything to have a friend, and if it was looking at our stupid cows, then I was OK with that.

"Cows!" Chad grumbled. "Big deal. Everyone around here has cows."

I led them across the yard to our corral. "We have only 10," I told the boys when we got to the fence. "Purebred Simmentals. They're due to calve in early March."

"Graham's dad has more than 200 cows," Chad said.

"Let's make Jet chase them," Graham suggested. "I want to see one of the McGinness dogs work."

I thought quickly. "We can't," I said.

"Why not?" Graham asked. He climbed up on the fence and sat on the top rail, his feet dangling over the edge.

" Because, uh—" I tried to come up with a good answer. "Because Dad's afraid it will hurt the cows."

Chad gave me a look before climbing up on the corral fence besides Graham. "How could it hurt the cows to be chased a bit?"

"Well, they are pregnant," I explained.

"Duh!" Chad said. "But they don't run on their stomachs now, do they?"

"Oh, just drop it," Graham said. "It's no big deal."

I breathed a sigh of relief.

Chad frowned. He slowly stood up on the top rail of the fence, balancing there. "Want to see my tightrope act?" he asked. He turned to the right, and took one slow step along the fence.

"Hey," I said, "you better get off."

"And who's gonna make me?" Chad challenged. He took another step forward, swaying back and forth.

I looked across the corral. Satan and the rest of the herd had walked forward when we had come into the corral, curious, I suppose, or hoping for a bite of hay or something else good to eat. Most of the cows had now backed up, but Satan wasn't in a very good mood when she saw we didn't have any food. She snorted and began to paw at the snow.

"You're going to hurt yourself," I warned. "The wood's slippery."

"I'm not going to fall," Chad said. "I'm a circus star." He took another step, then another.

Great. Chad was going to be a tightrope star on my corral, fall in, and be mauled by our killer cow. That was going to really help me earn friends at school, wasn't it?

"My dad's going to be mad," I yelled, taking a step backward. "Come on guys, let's go," I pleaded.

"In a minute," Chad said. "I've not finished my act yet." He was about halfway down the corral fence, moving faster and faster in an effort to keep his balance.

"Look, Chad," I said in my most reasonable tone.

"One of our cows is really nasty. I don't want you falling in there with her."

Chad glanced away from the fence for a moment. Satan looked at him and shook her head. "Oh, big deal! I've chased more cows than you'll ever see in your lifetime, Olsen. They're all bluff."

"That cow is not faking it," I said.

"What's the matter?" Chad asked. He stopped and rocked back and forth on the fence. "Don't tell me that big ol' nasty cow has little Marky-Warky scared!"

OK, I thought, *I won't tell him. If he's determined to risk his own life by walking on the top of our fence, so be it.*

Then Chad did a really stupid thing. I don't know if he slipped or if he jumped into the corral on purpose, but when I turned around Chad was standing inside the cattle pen.

"Hey!" I yelled. "Get out of there!"

Chad put his hands to his ears and fanned them at the red cow. "Hey, there, El Toro, nah-nah! Come and get me."

The red cow pawed the ground and snorted.

Chad put his head down and pawed the ground back.

Satan took a step forward and shook her head.

Chad shook his head and took a step toward her.

"Chad, you idiot!" Graham called. "Get out of there! That cow looks mad!"

"Do you think so?" Chad pawed the ground again

and took another step toward the cow. "Well, let's just see about that."

The big red cow didn't wait another second. She swung her head again and rushed straight at Chad. I hadn't realized until then how fast a cow could move. She came at the boy like a freight train at full throttle on a downhill track. Chad obviously didn't know how fast a cow could move either. He jumped backward, hoping to outrun Satan, but he didn't have a chance.

The red cow's wide forehead hit Chad at hip level. She flipped her head up, throwing the boy forward. Chad somersaulted through the air (he really would have made an excellent circus performer, after all) before landing on the frozen ground near the wooden fence.

But that wasn't enough for Satan. She spotted the boy lying there by the fence and pawed the ground again.

"Don't move!" Graham yelled.

"Run!" I bellowed.

Chad didn't listen to either one of us. He sat up slowly, staring at the cow with wide eyes.

Satan glared back at him and slowly advanced, snorting loudly.

Graham scrambled over the top rail of the corral, yelling loudly, "Get away; get away!" I was right behind him, waving my hands.

Satan wasn't the least bit intimidated. If anything, she seemed energized by this extra attention. I could almost hear her thinking, *Oh goody, I can now squish three boys instead of just one!*

I don't know what would have happened if Jet hadn't been there. At one moment he had been in the long grass near the barn, sniffing at some interesting smell. Then he must have seen what was happening. The little dog flew across the yard straight toward us. He slipped under the bottom board of the corral without slowing his pace and dashed over to Chad. He barked loudly, his tail held stiffly over his back.

Satan spun around, swinging her head at Jet.

"Go get her, boy!" I yelled. "Sic 'em!"

I had no idea what would happen. For the past two weeks I'd been trying to get Jet to chase the cows with no success at all. Why would today be any different?

Satan got her bearings and charged straight at Jet. At the last possible second Jet jumped to the side. As the cow rushed past him, Jet jumped forward and nipped at her back legs. She kicked out at the dog but he ducked, her feet skimming over Jet's back with inches to spare.

"Come on, Chad!" Graham hissed. "Get out of there."

This time Chad didn't hesitate. He scrambled to his feet and began to frantically clamber up the corral. When Satan saw her victim disappearing, she spun around and whirled back toward Chad, her eyes narrow and angry.

"Watch out!" I screamed.

The big cow was almost upon Chad when Jet caught up with her. He jumped forward, catching the cow's tail in his mouth and biting down. Satan let out a terrible bellow and twirled around. Jet twirled around too, desperately hanging on to the cow's tail. He flew through the air wildly, his feet pawing at the air for traction, but it didn't help.

The cow bellowed and spun around the opposite way. Jet's teeth must have lost their grip, because he suddenly shot through the air like a rocket.

Chad hurled himself over the top rail of the corral and landed in a heap at our feet. He was safe. A moment later Jet trotted around the corral, his tail wagging happily. I noticed that his white ruff was now covered with cow manure, but the dog didn't seem worried.

"Good boy!" I praised the little dog. I rubbed his back enthusiastically, being careful to avoid the dirty spots.

Jet smiled modestly, his tongue lolling out of his mouth as he accepted my praise. After all, even heroes like a compliment now and then.

Finally Chad stood up and wiped snow off the back of his blue jeans. "Wow!" he said. "That was exciting!"

"Exciting!" I gasped. "You almost got killed."

"Yeah, I did, didn't I?" Chad drawled.

"Idiot!" Graham shot at him, but he was smiling.

Jet trotted over to Chad, his lips curled back in a doggy smile. Chad hesitated before slowly reaching over and giving Jet a pat. "Good dog," he praised. "Thanks."

Jet waved his tail proudly, then raced over for his stick. He brought it back to Chad and dropped it at the boy's feet.

"You gotta play fetch with him now," I warned the boy.

"Why?"

"That's his reward for saving your life, stupid," Graham said. "You always have to reward your rescuer."

"Oh." Chad gingerly picked up the stick. "Yuck. Dog slobber," he said. "Gross." He threw the stick across the yard.

Jet wagged his tail happily and raced after the stick. He had known all along that the nice boy would want to play with him. A dog simply has to time it right.

"You guys better not tell anyone what happened," Chad muttered, throwing Jet's stick again. "My old man would kill me."

"I won't say a word," I promised.

"Me neither," Graham said.

Chad looked at me, then held out his hand. "Friends?" he said.

I put my fist on top of Chad's, and Graham put his on top of mine. "Friends," I declared.

Jet dropped the stick on top of Chad's toe. "Hey, watch it, dog," Chad said with a grin.

"Jet wants to be your friend, too," I told the boys.

Chad wiped his hand on his pant leg. "With friends like Jet," he said, grinning, "who needs an enemy?"

Jet barked and wagged his tail. Then he whirled around and raced across the yard after a flock of sparrows. His job as a cow dog was over. Now he could go back to the really fun things: birds!

8

The Accident

The unusually warm weather continued all week. By the middle of February the snow had shrunk down to almost nothing. I guess that's why Dad decided this was the perfect time to haul in the last of Grandpa's straw bales.

"We're going to need all the straw we can get," Dad said that morning as he slipped into his snowsuit.

"Why?" I asked. I wasn't too thrilled as I pulled my own ski pants on. I could think of a lot of better things to do than help Dad haul bales. Chad had phoned this morning, asking if I could come over later, and Dad had made me turn him down.

The two boys were much friendlier now. I had gone over to Graham's house the week before, and both boys phoned me occasionally.

And Jet was still a big part of my day. He was more fun than anything had been in the city. In fact, we had just started something new in the past week. I had taught Jet to pull me behind him on my skis. Jet could get his speed up pretty well when we were on the hard packed snow in the lane, and although we wouldn't turn the direction I wanted, he would stop when I hollered "Whoa!" Then the warm weather put an end to our skiing.

Anyhow, I wasn't that thrilled with Dad's bale project. But he insisted that he needed my help that day.

"We'll need lots of fresh bedding when the cows start calving," Dad explained.

I rolled my eyes, but tried not to grumble too much. Which wasn't easy for a complainer such as me. I knew from experience that once my dad gets an idea, things aren't about to change. Besides, I hoped that if we finished early maybe I could still go over to Chad's house.

"Do you think this piece of junk will work?" I asked Dad as we hooked the tractor up to a big old wooden wagon that had been parked behind the barn.

"It's not in very good shape," Dad admitted, looking at the floor of the wagon. "But I imagine it will carry a few loads."

"Can I drive?" I asked.

Dad shook his head. "No way. We're going to take the tractor down the road, and you don't have a license."

"I'll be a good driver," I argued.

"Right," Dad said. "This from the kid who can hardly walk and chew gum at the same time!"

"That's mean!" I laughed. "Mean, but true."

Dad motioned for me to climb on the wagon. The tractor started with a roar, and we headed down the road toward the field where the straw bales were stacked.

Jet was delighted to have some outside company. At first he rode on the wagon beside me. When that was too slow, he jumped off and raced around in the ditch beside the road as the tractor steadily chugged along.

Loading the straw bales was hard work. Dad stood on the ground and tossed the bales up to me on the wagon. My job was to haul and stack the bales into position. Dad showed me the trick of overlapping the bales so they stayed upright.

"It's almost the same as making a Lego house," Dad explained. "You see? If you put one bale directly on top of the other it will be unsteady and tip easily. You need to lay your bottom layer of bales this direction, and then the next layer of bales the other way."

I grunted and groaned as I dragged the big straw bales across the wagon floor. The work got harder as I moved up to each higher layer. Before long I had to climb several bale steps to reach the top row.

"You know, I don't want to complain," I said. "But—"

"Then don't," Dad interrupted me. He wiped a bead of sweat off his forehead and tossed another bale up beside me.

"Isn't there a child labor law?" I protested. "I'm sure you're breaking it."

"Could be," Dad grinned. His snowsuit and knit hat were covered with straw, but he seemed remarkably cheerful. "And when we get back home you have one last job to do."

"What?"

"Build a doghouse," Dad said.

I groaned loudly. "I am going to report you for this," I threatened. "My back's killing me."

"You'll live," Dad said unsympathetically.

"I don't think so," I groaned.

"Consider yourself lucky," Dad said. "We could be hauling hay today instead of straw."

"A bale is a bale," I said.

"Mark, these straw bales weigh 40 pounds, at most. Hay bales can be twice that heavy."

"Eighty pounds!" I yelled. "You don't think I could move 80-pound bales, do you?"

"You'd be slower," Dad admitted, "but you'd manage."

"Tomorrow I'm staying in the house," I said. "I'll help Mom with the sewing and baking and stuff like that."

"Your mom doesn't sew," Dad pointed out.

"That's why she needs me," I said. "And maybe Ryan can come out to help you."

Dad laughed. "I imagine he'd be a big help."

We rested for a few minutes, watching Jet race

from one stack of bales to the next. Jet had discovered something new to chase. Families of mice were nesting under some of the bales. Jet hadn't caught one yet, but he had come close.

At least mice don't fly, I thought with a smile. *Jet might even have a chance of catching one of them.*

I climbed to the top of the bale stack and flopped on my belly for the ride home. Dad waved at me and called something that I couldn't hear very well over the noise of the tractor. We headed down the road toward home.

It was kind of fun riding on the load of straw. I had a good view of the surrounding fields and ditches. The straw was cozy, but did rock a bit. I hoped that I had done a good enough job stacking bales. I wouldn't want the whole thing to come tumbling down and dump me out on the road.

Jet raced along beside the tractor, his ears pricked forward and his tail busily wagging. He had enjoyed the adventure. Of course, it was easy for him, I decided. No one expected a dog to lift 40-pound bales.

We were only a mile or so from home when it happened.

Dad was driving the tractor on the right-hand side of the road. Jet was running ahead of him and slightly to the right, so he was almost in the ditch.

Suddenly I saw Jet's ears prick up. He sprang forward with a bounce and scooted to the left, disappearing under the wheels of the tractor! There was a thump, and the front wheel of the tractor bounced upward, as though it had struck something. Then the back wheel of the tractor rose up.

Dad had run over Jet!

I let out a scream and started to stand up on the load of straw.

Dad slammed on the brakes. The tractor and wagon came to a sudden halt. The load of straw, with me on top of it, kept traveling forward. Several of the top bales tumbled over the front of the wagon onto the hard ground below. I grabbed wildly at the nearest bales, trying to slow my fall. I hit the ground with a *thud,* straw bales tumbling around me. The frozen ground was hard, and I ripped a hole in the knee of my snow pants when I hit the road.

I wasn't seriously hurt. But what had happened to Jet? I had seen him disappear under the tractor wheels, but I couldn't see him now. Where was he?

Dad was standing besides me. His face was pale. "He ran straight out in front of me," Dad said, "after a mouse that came out of the ditch." His voice was shaking.

"Where is he?" I asked. I was almost scared to look.

We bent to look under the wagon. Nothing was there.

"Is he under the bales?" I asked, looking at the dozen or so straw bales that lay scattered between the tractor and wagon.

"I don't know," Dad said. He grabbed at the bales,

jerking them out of the way.

But Jet wasn't there, either.

"Jet," I called, scanning the ditch frantically. A black dog should be easy to see against the white snow. But there was nothing dark in the ditch except a lump of dirt near the bushes.

A lump of dirt? With a sickening feeling I hurried toward the lump. *Dear God, don't let that be my dog. Please!*

It was Jet. His eyes fluttered and opened as I ran up to him. He looked bewildered. Surprised. Confused.

"Jet!" I cried.

Jet lifted his head and shoulders and tried to stand. But as soon as his back end moved, he let out a shrill howl and flopped over on his side. His eyes were wide and frightened.

"What's wrong, boy?" I asked. I looked at Jet carefully. There seemed to be a streak or two of bright red intertwined in the long black hair on his legs. But I couldn't see any deep cuts or injuries.

"It's OK," I told the dog.

But it wasn't. How could anything be run over by a tractor and be OK?

Jet let out another whimper and arched his back. He began to shake and tremble, his whole body vibrating on the cold snow beneath him.

Dad reached forward to touch Jet, and then jerked his hand away. "We have to take Jet to the vet," Dad said.

"Hurry!" I pleaded.

Jet began to scream. It was a horrible sound and made both Dad and me jump to our feet in panic.

"OK, Mark," Dad said. "You stay with Jet. I'll run home and get the car."

Dad began to jog away. He had gone only a few steps when he stopped and spun around. "What am I doing?" he shouted. "The tractor will be faster." Dad clambered up the tractor and slipped it into gear. The tires spun as Dad lurched forward. Suddenly he came to a stop and scrambled down from the tractor seat and jogged over to me.

"Here, take my coat," Dad said. He pulled it off and carefully laid it over Jet. "I'll be back as quickly as I can."

When Dad was out of sight I sank down in the snow by Jet. I pulled the coat back far enough so that I could see Jet's face. He had quit screaming, but now he was panting as though it was a hot summer day. His eyes were opened wide with pain and fear. He made another attempt to sit up, but as soon as he moved he gave a shriek and flopped over in the snow. His front paws moved back and forth as though he was swimming, but he kept his back legs still.

I felt sick to my stomach. "God, please don't let Jet be hurt too bad."

I wanted to be in the house with Mom. I wanted to be anywhere but here. It hurt me to see Jet writhe with pain beside me.

And there was nothing that I could do. Except pray.

It was probably the most sincere and honest prayer that I had ever made. I mean, a lot of my prayers are lazy ones, about little things that I really don't need. This prayer was different. I begged God to save Jet's life. I begged him to make Jet feel better. And I begged Him to help Dad get here soon.

My pastor says we're supposed to pray and leave it in God's hands to answer in the way that He thinks best. But at that moment I couldn't honestly ask God to do anything but help us.

After about a million years Dad drove up with the car. He parked straight across from us and hopped out, carrying a blanket. Together we carefully slid Jet onto the blanket and lifted him onto the back seat of the car. Then we raced off to the nearest veterinarian clinic.

Jet was still alive when we got there. Dr. Solick was preparing to operate on a cat when we staggered into the clinic, carrying Jet between us on the blanket. The receptionist called Dr. Solick up front to see us. He took one look at Jet and peeled his surgical gloves off. "Guess our little tomcat's going to get off easy today," the vet said. "He can wait. Let's look at what you've got here."

First Dr. Solick gave Jet an injection of medicine for pain. "Our first priority is a good, clear set of X-rays," the vet said. "Although I have a pretty good idea what we're going to see." He pointed to Jet's back legs and shook his head. Before too long Dr. Solick motioned for Dad and me to come back to the examining room.

"I'd like you to look at this," Dr. Solick said. He wasn't smiling.

The vet put the X-ray pictures in front of a bright light. "Not this one," Dr. Solick said, slipping one X-ray out of the way. "Look here, at Jet's back legs."

"What is it?"

"His left leg is fine, just a few lacerations," Dr. Solick said. "But compare it to this picture. You'll see that the entire set of bones are shattered."

The leg looked like a jigsaw puzzle. Hundreds of tiny bone fragments shone on the X-ray negatives instead of the solid bones that should have been there.

"Can it be repaired?" Dad asked.

Dr. Solick sighed. "That's the million-dollar question," he said.

"What do you mean?"

"This bone is far beyond anything I can repair," Dr. Solick said. "I don't know if the university veterinary clinic in Edmonton could do anything, but I certainly can't. There isn't enough healthy bone left."

"We love this dog," Dad said softly.

"I know you do," Dr. Solick said. "But he's suffering a lot right now."

"What do you suggest?" Dad asked slowly.

"Well, I think you have three choices. First, you could choose to take him to the University of Alberta veterinary clinic. I could phone ahead and prepare them for your coming. They have a much more specialized clinic and the equipment. But I don't give them much chance for success."

"It would hurt Jet to be moved, wouldn't it?" I asked.

Dr. Solick nodded his head. "We could give him more painkiller," he said, "but yes, he's still going to be very uncomfortable."

"You said three options," Dad said. "Let's hear the other two."

"You could have me put him down now." Dr. Solick said the words softly.

"Put him down!" I felt as though I'd been socked in the chest.

Dr. Solick laid his hand on my shoulder. "He's in a terrible amount of pain, son," Dr. Solick said. "And if we can't help him, we can't leave him to suffer, either."

My eyes filled with tears, and I suddenly didn't care if anyone saw it.

"What's your third suggestion?" Dad asked tiredly.

"We could amputate his right leg," Dr. Solick said.

"Amputate Jet's leg?" I gasped.

Dr. Solick nodded his head. "That's actually the suggestion that I think makes the most sense. He's a young dog, and he should heal well."

"Jet's a Border collie," I said, still staring at the X-ray in front of me. "He'll be miserable if he can't move and run."

"Most dogs learn to move well with three legs,"

Dr. Solick said. "When I was a kid we had a three-legged dog who did everything. But it takes time."

"Well, we can't just shoot him," I said. I stood up and turned away from the men and wiped my eyes. "We don't shoot people if they get hurt, do we? So we can't shoot Jet."

"I wouldn't shoot Jet," the vet said softly. "I would give him an injection of medication that would put him to sleep."

"I don't care," I said. "I don't want him to die."

"Then I think you should consider amputation," Dr. Solick said. He turned to my dad. "I honestly don't believe that the university will be able to repair Jet's leg. It's been crushed into millions of bone fragments. My recommendation is that you allow me to amputate his leg at the hip."

"Would he get better?" Dad asked.

Dr. Solick shrugged. "I can't promise you anything," he said. "But he doesn't appear to have any internal injuries. I must warn you that it's going to cost you a fair amount of money, and your dog will have to stay at the clinic for a week or so. And it's possible that he will never get better."

"Can we have a few minutes to think about this?" Dad asked.

"I want to see Jet," I said.

"Certainly," Dr. Solick said. "This is a serious decision, and I want you to have a chance to think about it. Come see your dog, and think about it. Pray about it."

"That's what I intend to do," Dad said. "Thank you, Doctor."

Jet was sprawled out on the examining table. His brown eyes were open a slit, and they had a strange, glassy appearance to them. I lifted one hand and very gently touched Jet's face. I didn't know if Jet would realize I was there, but he did. His tongue came out and he licked me on the hand.

"Let's pray, son," Dad said. He took my hand, and we bowed our heads.

We asked God to help us know what was best for Jet. We asked Him to take away Jet's pain and help him not be so afraid. And we prayed that God would give Dr. Solick wisdom and knowledge so that he could do the very best possible thing for Jet.

When we were finished praying, I saw Dad wipe a tear away from his face. I was shocked. I don't remember ever seeing my dad cry before. It made me feel a bit better knowing that my dad loved Jet, too. *I hate dogs*, Dad had said. But he didn't hate this dog.

"I think we should let Dr. Solick amputate his leg," Dad finally said.

"That's what I want too," I said slowly. "But Dad, I'm scared."

"Are you scared he's going to die?"

"No—I mean, yes, I'm scared Jet's gong to die. But I'm also scared that he'll live and hate his life. Grandpa said that Border collies can't live if they can't run."

"What does Grandpa know?" Dad said fiercely.

"I don't know," I said. "But it worries me."

"Let's try to save Jet's life," Dad said. "We can worry about how he feels later."

"But Dad—"

"We can send him to counseling later," Dad said, attempting to smile. "In case he has any unresolved issues over being a three-legged dog."

"That's not funny, Dad."

"I know," he said. "But I don't know what else to say."

"Where will you get the money?"

"I'll sell one of the cows, if necessary," Dad said. He smiled faintly. "That red one that chased you boys the other day."

I blinked. "You knew about that?" I asked.

He nodded his head. "Your mom saw it happen," he said.

"Why didn't you say anything?"

"We figured you boys learned an important lessons on your own," Dad said. "But it really wouldn't hurt my feelings if I had to sell that cow."

I touched Jet with one finger and watched as his tail wagged faintly.

"OK, Dad," I said. "You've got a deal. Let Dr. Solick take off Jet's leg."

I began to cry again. But this time Dad took me in his arms and pulled me close. We stood like that for a long time. And I'm not too old to admit that it felt good.

I'm glad I have a dad who cares for me. And I'm glad that God cares enough for us that He would listen to our prayers about a little black dog that lay on the examining table in front of us.

9

The Three-legged Dog

I didn't visit the veterinarian clinic the next day. Dr. Solick said that Jet would be sleeping most of the time, anyway. "He's doing as well as can be expected, but there's no use seeing him," Dr. Solick told me when I'd phoned the next afternoon. "Let him have today to recover."

To be honest, I was a bit relieved. I missed Jet, and I was worried about him, but I was also scared to see him.

Jet had been so handsome—so alive and vibrant and busy. What would he be like now? A three-legged dog . . . A sad and sore three-legged dog. It was almost too much to imagine.

We drove over after school on Tuesday.

"He's a bit better today," Dr. Solick said as he led us through the main part of the building into the back. "But he's still pretty sleepy. We're keeping him quite sedated."

A variety of different-sized cages filled the back room of the clinic. Several cats howled from the far wall, but I didn't pay any attention to them. A German shepherd puppy stood on his hind legs and pawed through the cage bars at us, but I hurried past it, too.

Where was Jet?

"Here," Dr. Solick said, bending over and unfastening the far cage. "Here's your boy."

Jet was sleeping on an old piece of carpet at the back of the cage. The cage was large and clean, but the bowl of dog food in the front of it was untouched. I looked at the dish and the cage and the carpet for a long time, trying to avoid looking at Jet.

Finally I couldn't wait any longer.

It wasn't as bad as I had expected. There was no blood. No gore. Just a small sleeping dog with a thick white bandage covering his hip.

Jet seemed smaller somehow, as though he had shrunk like Alice in Wonderland did after eating the magic potion. The cage was big and lonely, and Jet seemed almost lost in it. His eyes were closed, and his breathing was deep. As I watched, his long collie nose with the perfect white blaze twitched. The black hairs over his eyes wiggled, and then he was still again. So still.

This wasn't the Jet I knew. The real Jet was always running, always chasing something, always looking for attention. And now he was changed. I hadn't realized that his accident would change him like that.

Jet wouldn't ever be my trick dog now. He wouldn't jump through hoops or push baby carriages or pull me on my skis. I felt a moment's sadness, and then I shrugged it away. Jet was still alive. That was all that mattered for now.

I bent down by the cage, and put my hand carefully on Jet's shoulder. "Jet," I said softly. "Hey, boy."

Jet's eyes opened. He blinked several times, and then his nose quivered.

"It's me, Jet," I said, rubbing the thick ruff of white hair around his neck and shoulders.

Jet raised his head cautiously and looked at me. His ears pricked forward for a moment, and his tail wagged once.

My eyes darted again to Jet's legs. One back leg was shaved close and looked naked with its short stubble of hair. A small line of stitches ran up the outside of the leg. The other leg was gone. I had known that, of course, but it still seemed strange. Luckily, there was nothing gross to see. A heavy bandage wound around Jet's right hip, across his waist, and back to his hip again. Beyond the bandage there was nothing.

Just a sleeping dog with something not quite right. Something missing.

Poor Jet.

"He looks awful." Dad spoke for the first time, making me jump. I had almost forgotten that he had come in with me.

"Well, he has been feeling pretty low," the vet said. "Isn't eating anything to speak of. It will be good for him to have some company."

"He isn't eating at all?" Dad asked.

"That's to be expected," Dr. Solick said. "He's still in a lot of pain, and the medications make him sleep much of the day. It doesn't take much to make an animal depressed."

"Can dogs get depressed?" Dad asked in surprise.

"Why, certainly," Dr. Solick said. "If they're lonely, frightened, or hurt they tend to withdraw."

"I didn't know that," Dad said.

I sat down on the cold cement floor and began to rub Jet's muzzle. He pushed his face toward me and closed his eyes. His tail wagged again, and he parted his lips in a faint smile.

"Let me tell you a true story," Dr. Solick said. "A family once brought me a parrot to keep an eye on while they went on summer holidays. There were four kids in the family, who had spent hours tormenting the poor bird—poking things through the wires of the cage and just generally bugging it. The parents thought the parrot would be happy to have a holiday of its own. But do you know what happened? As soon as they were gone the parrot quit eating and drinking. In fact, I began to worry that it was going to die."

"What did you do?" I asked.

"I phoned the family, and they suggested I bang on the bird's cage."

"What!"

"That's right," Dr. Solick said. "Every morning and evening we'd bang on the cage and poke things through the bars, and yell and make a lot of noise. As soon as that old parrot heard all the commotion he woke right up. Started to eat everything in sight. He was a new bird after that—as long as we kept up the noise and activity!"

"Are you telling us the truth?" I asked.

"Scout's honor," Dr. Solick said, raising his right hand.

"You're not a Boy Scout," I laughed.

Dr. Solick grinned. "No, I'm not," he said. "But I'm still telling you the truth. My point is, animals—and people, too—don't do very well when they're out of their normal environment. They tend to improve once they're back home."

Jet's eyes were closed, but his thick black tail continued to wave back and forth as I stroked his side.

"What should we do for Jet?" Dad asked.

"There isn't much you can do for a few days," Dr. Solick said. "But come visit him as often as you can. If all goes well, you can take him home on Friday."

"I'll come tomorrow," I told the vet. "And maybe I can bring his pillow from home. That might make him feel better."

"Good idea," Dr. Solick agreed. "And bring some of his own dog food, too. Anything you think he'd like."

Dr. Solick excused himself and left the room. Dad paced around the small area and finally sank down on the cement near me. He didn't touch Jet, but his eyes gently studied the dog.

Before long Jet fell back asleep. Dad stood up and motioned to me. "Let's go," he whispered.

Jet opened his eyes and looked at Dad.

"Do I have to?" I asked.

"I'll bring you again tomorrow," Dad said. "Let Jet rest now."

"It's time for me to go," I told the dog. Jet raised his head and looked at me. His tail quit wagging, but his eyes were still bright.

"I'll be back tomorrow," I said. "Honest." I stood up stiffly and rubbed my back. Tomorrow I'd bring Jet's pillow—and sit on it while I was visiting him.

Dad reached over and scratched Jet's forehead. "Poor old fellow," Dad said softly. "I hope we did the right thing for you."

"He's going to be OK," I said. "We just need to get him home."

"You know, I was just kidding," Dad said.

"About what?"

"When I said that we'd send Jet for counseling," Dad replied. "I honestly didn't know that dogs could get depressed." Dad looked sad himself.

"It's going to be OK," I repeated. "Don't worry, Dad. I think we did the right thing."

When I got to the doorway, I looked back at Jet.

He attempted to stand up. He stumbled and fell sideways, striking the cage wall with his side. He whimpered, then lay quietly, watching us go.

The winter wind was sharp and brought tears to my eyes when we stepped outside. If only I could sit down with Jet and explain everything to him. I'd tell him that I wasn't leaving for good, that I'd be back tomorrow. I'd tell him that the doctor was going to make him feel better, and that it wouldn't always be like this. That one day he'd be able to walk again. I hoped.

But Jet didn't speak English, and I didn't speak dog language. So I'd just have to leave things in God's hands. Jet would be home in a few days.

The picture of Jet stumbling in the little cage was burned into my memory. What had we done to our dog? Would this be his life, stumbling and struggling to move? No wonder Grandpa was so sad all the time. Just seeing Jet helped me understand Grandpa's situation better. It wasn't just losing a leg. It was realizing that you were a different dog—a different person—now.

And it wasn't a change for the better.

10

The Marvelous Mouth Strikes Again

I've got to run to the seed cleaning plant," Dad said after our visit to Jet the next day. "I need to pick up some mineral for the cows and see about getting some grain crushed for them to eat."

"Will that take long?" I asked.

Dad shrugged. "Hard to say. It depends how many people are ahead of me."

"Can I visit Grandpa?" I asked.

Dad looked surprised. "Sure," he said. "That would be fine."

In a few minutes we pulled up at the hospital's front entry. "I'll come in and get you when I've finished my business," Dad said. "I'll probably be gone for at least a half hour or so."

"That's OK," I said. I clambered out of the car.

"Mark," Dad said. Then he hesitated.

"What?"

"Are you going to tell Grandpa about Jet?"

I thought for a moment. "I don't know," I finally said. "Shouldn't I tell him?"

Dad sighed. "I don't know," he admitted. "It might make him pretty upset."

"Well, he's going to find out eventually," I said. "I mean, Grandpa's legs might not work very well, but there's nothing wrong with his eyes! When I walk into the hospital with a three-legged dog he's bound to notice."

Dad smiled faintly. "I know," he said. "I know. But just be prepared. He might be rather upset."

I walked through the hospital sliding doors, still uncertain what to do.

God, I'm just a kid. And I don't know what to say or think. I mean, I'm having a hard time dealing with Jet's accident myself. How do I know what to say to Grandpa?

I hoped that this time God would give me some better inspiration than He had during my last visit with Grandpa. Otherwise, I was going to have to wing it on my own. And I already knew that I wasn't so good at saying the right thing at the right time. Marvelous Mark Olsen and the Mighty Moving Mouth. Ha! I was better at putting my foot in my mouth than anything else.

Grandpa's room door was closed tightly. I knocked on it, then pushed the door open a few inches.

"Who is it?" Grandpa called. Even from a distance his voice sounded impatient.

I hesitated for a moment, and then smiled to myself. "It's the Avon lady," I called in a high girlie voice.

There was a pause. Then Grandpa's voice called again. "Look, lady," he said, "I told you yesterday— no more lipstick! That color just doesn't look good on me."

"Grandpa!" I pushed open the door and rushed into the room.

Grandpa was sitting on the edge of the bed. He grinned a crooked grin at me. "Hey, you're not the Avon lady," he said.

"How can you be so sure, Grandpa?" I asked, grinning back.

"Your legs are too hairy," Grandpa said. "And you smell like a dog."

"Grandpa!"

"Well, you do."

"I'd rather smell like a dog than a cow," I retorted. "Remember how Jet stunk when we brought him home from McGinness's?"

"Where is that mangy mutt, anyhow?" Grandpa said. His eyes darted around the room, and then he looked back at me.

"I didn't bring him," I said.

"Why not?" Grandpa frowned, and his forehead wrinkled in a perfect letter W.

"You'll have to put up with me," I told Grandpa. "I'm better looking than Jet anyway!"

"I wouldn't go that far," Grandpa said, but the wrinkles on his forehead relaxed a bit.

"I'm not as hairy," I said with a grin, sinking down on the bed beside Grandpa.

"I don't hold it against you," Grandpa said. "And maybe you'll improve as you age."

I laughed. Grandpa seemed almost like his old self today. I noticed that he'd had his hair cut recently, and the untidy crop of stubble on his face was gone. Grandpa was paying attention to his looks. He was getting better.

Grandpa seemed to know what I was thinking. He looked at me, then pointed at the wheelchair that was across the room. "Bring that over here, Mark," he ordered.

I marched across the room and grabbed the wheelchair by the handles. I gave it a firm push but the chair barely budged.

"Hey there, wise guy," Grandpa laughed. "Why don't you undo the brakes?"

"Good idea," I said. I struggled for a moment with the brakes and finally got the wheelchair to roll properly.

"It scares me," Grandpa said.

"What?"

"To think that you'll have your driver's license in a few years," Grandpa teased. "You can't even manage a wheelchair."

I rolled my eyes. "Where do you want me to put the chair, Grandpa?" I asked.

"Right here by the bed."

I rolled the wheelchair into position and snapped the brakes back on.

"Watch this," Grandpa said. He stood up beside the bed.

I quickly stepped forward to take Grandpa's arm, but Grandpa shrugged me away. Grandpa's legs were shaky, but he stood upright for a minute. Then he reached forward and grabbed hold of one side of the wheelchair with his hand. He pivoted awkwardly, shifting his weight from one foot to the other, until the wheelchair was straight behind him. Then he slowly dragged his feet backward. When the wheelchair was right against his backside, he bent over and sat down.

"All right, Grandpa!" I cheered. "You can walk!"

"I wouldn't call that a walk," Grandpa said from the wheelchair. "But it's a step in the right direction. Get it? A step in the right direction."

"That's terrific!"

"You have no idea how much better I feel now that I can do that," Grandpa said. "Just a few steps makes a big difference. Today I sat in a real chair when we had dinner, instead of this stupid wheelchair. And better yet, I took myself to the can for the first time all winter."

"Way to go, Grandpa!"

"Look, kid," Grandpa said, "sometimes it's the little things that really matter. Like a trip to the bathroom."

I rolled my eyes. "Thanks for sharing that."

Grandpa rolled the wheelchair my direction, stopping in front of me as I sat on the edge of his bed. "You helped me, kiddo," he said with a faint smile.

"I didn't do a thing," I replied quickly.

"Mark, I haven't been myself all winter," Grandpa said. "You're just a kid, and I don't want to burden you with my problems. But I do want you to know that just having you around has helped."

"How?"

Grandpa shrugged. "I'm not sure. And I don't want to get all mushy. But having a young person around with lots of life and energy helped. Plus, I have to admit that seeing Jet was good for me, too. A dog is a taste of the outdoors."

"I knew it," I said. "I could tell you liked Jet."

"I've always liked dogs," Grandpa agreed. "And even though Jet is a lousy cow dog, I still admire his joy of life. He loves to run, to be free. I guess that helped me see that's the way I still want to be."

"Wow." I thought about that for a moment. "I guess God did answer my prayers, Grandpa."

"God?"

"When Jet and I were here last time I prayed that God would help me say the right things to cheer you up."

"I don't know whether God had anything to do with it," Grandpa said. "I don't believe that He has time to worry about everyone all the time."

"He does," I said firmly.

"Mark, I believe in God," Grandpa Olsen said just as firmly. "I know that the world wasn't created by accident; there must have been a Master Planner. Any farmer can tell that nature has an order and design to it that couldn't have been just an accident."

"I know!"

"But Mark, I don't believe that God runs out and talks to people and makes them do certain stuff, and all," Grandpa continued. "He made people, and then keeps out of their lives."

"God talks to me," I said.

"You've heard God talk to you?"

I hesitated. "Well, not exactly talk to me, but I know that He's there in my life."

"How?"

"Well, He helps me be brave when I have problems. I feel different when I pray. Better, somehow."

Grandpa sighed. "I guess this is just one area where we'll have to agree to disagree, son. I don't think you're likely to change a stubborn old coot like me."

"Something bad has happened to Jet," I suddenly blurted.

Don't ask me how that got in the middle of our conversation. Until then I hadn't even decided if I was going to tell Grandpa about Jet's accident. On hindsight it certainly didn't seem like the most appropriate time to pop that information into our discussion. But the words rushed out of me like water down the bathtub drain, and once I'd pulled the plug, so to speak, it was too late to stop.

"What happened?"

"He ran under the tractor after a mouse," I said. "His back leg got crushed."

"Is he dead?" Grandpa asked. His voice sounded sad.

I shook my head. "He's at the vet clinic."

"Is he going to be OK?"

I didn't say anything. In fact, I had to blink hard to keep the tears back.

Was Jet going to be OK? Had we done the right thing for him? It was hard to say. And I certainly didn't have the answers.

11

Things Begin to Look Up

I visited Jet every afternoon after school. Graham offered to come with me once, but I turned him down. I didn't want anyone to see Jet the way he was now.

He still wasn't walking. He wasn't even trying to stand up. Dr. Solick told me it was nothing to worry about, but the look on his face said differently.

Jet had never been a very heavy dog—too much running and chasing after birds and boys, I guess. But now he was even thinner.

"He's really not eating very much," Dr. Solick had explained.

I had been able to get Jet to take a bit of food from my hand. And once he had squirmed his way over to me so that I could pet him easier. Other than that he really hadn't done anything but limply lay there in the cage.

On Friday afternoon Dad and I came with the car to take Jet home.

"Let's hope he snaps out of this once he gets to his own place," Dr. Solick said with a sigh. He gave Jet's head one last scratch. "If you have any further problems just phone me. Bring him back Monday, and we'll change that dressing again."

"Thanks a lot, Dr. Solick," I said.

Dad carefully scooped Jet up and carried him out to the car.

Jet's head came up when he got out into the fresh air. His nose twitched and his ears pricked forward with interest as he looked around the busy parking lot.

Dad settled Jet onto the blanket that covered the car's back seat. I slid in beside Jet. He lifted Jet's head up on my lap and fastened my seat belt.

"We're off," Dad said, turning the key in the ignition.

"I'm sure Jet will be glad to get out of the veterinarian clinic," I said, petting the dog's shoulder.

"I'm glad he's out, too," Dad said. "I was getting worried that I'd have to sell the farm to pay his vet bills."

"Jet's worth it," I said, studying the little dog carefully.

Dad nodded his head. "Yes," Dad said. "He is."

When we got home Dad and I carried Jet into the entryway and set him down on his pillow bed.

"How's he doing?" Mom asked, peering around the corner. She held Ryan in her arms, keeping the little boy from climbing into the entryway.

"He's not very good yet," I told Mom. "But I think he'll get better now that he's home."

"I know what it's like to be homesick," Mom said. "Iit doesn't feel very good."

"We'll really have to be sure to keep Ryan away from Jet," I warned Mom, glaring at the little boy. "Jet's leg is going to be sore for a long time, and Ryan could really hurt him."

Mom nodded her head. "I'm sure you're right," she said. "It's a good thing that it's so nice outside. Jet can spend much of the day on the deck, soaking up the sunshine."

"Outside?" I complained. "Why does he have to go outside?"

"Because it's against the law for me to lock your baby brother outside," Mom said with a smile. "And we have to keep the two of them apart somehow."

"Jet will freeze," I said.

"The sunshine will be good for him," Dad interrupted. "And he's an outdoor dog, anyway. I think he'll enjoy watching everything going on around him."

I frowned. "But Dad, you know that I haven't finished the doghouse yet."

"*Finished* the doghouse? Why, Mark, you haven't even *started* it yet."

"I don't have any wood," I said quickly.

"You do now," Dad said. "I picked up a load while you were at school today."

"Really?"

"Really," Dad repeated. "And I got nails and everything else you'll possibly need. So don't plan on going very far for the next few days, Mark. No more trips to Graham's place until Jet's doghouse is finished."

I looked at Mom desperately. "Mom!"

"Jet can sleep in the house tonight," she said. "It's almost Ryan's bedtime anyway. But we expect you to spend Sunday working on the doghouse."

I groaned. "What kind of heartless people are you? You'd put a poor, sick dog like Jet outside in the cold!"

Dad shook his head. "Mark, the weather has been beautiful all week. Jet will be fine—*if* you make a decent doghouse."

I turned to look at my dog. He was asleep on his old pillow, his nose tucked between his paws. I watched his calm, even breaths. Was it my imagination, or did Jet look a bit better already? But how would *I* look by the end of the weekend? My thumb would probably be mashed flat by my hammer. I wondered if Jet appreciated all the things I did for him.

🦴 🦴 🦴

I got up a bit early Sabbath morning and pulled on my old farm clothes before hiking down to the entryway. Jet was still lying on his pillow, but I thought the level of food in his dish was lower than it had been the evening before.

"Come on, Jet," I said, struggling to pick the dog up. "You need to go out to the bathroom."

I finally managed to get Jet outside. When he had finished, I carefully carried him back to the deck. I set him down in a sunny spot and stood back to look at the little dog.

Jet did seem a bit brighter. He was holding his head upright, and his eyes were sparkling as he looked around the yard. I began to scratch him in his favorite spots—under his neck, on his back, on his soft black chest. Jet sighed and closed his eyes. His tail began to wave back and forth slowly.

"Can't you growl anymore?" I asked.

He smiled up at me but didn't make a sound.

I was still petting Jet when the sudden flicker of wings overhead made me look up.

Mom had finally found our old birdfeeder in one of the moving boxes. Only the day before she had filled it with sunflower seeds and hung it from the entryway eaves. The chickadees had quickly discovered the birdseed, and they were lined up on the roof, waiting for their turn at the feeder.

Jet looked at the row of birds. His head lifted a bit higher and his tail began to move quicker.

"You can't fly," I informed the dog. "So don't even try."

He curled his lips back and laughed at me with bright eyes.

Mom knocked on the patio doors. "Time for breakfast," she called. Her voice was muffled through the windowpane, but I could still hear Ryan behind her, yelling at the birds. He held a piece of toast in one hand and pounded on the glass with another, leaving greasy handprints behind.

"Be a good dog," I told Jet. I gave him one last pat, then slipped inside. I quickly washed my hands and slid up to the breakfast table.

I had finished two pieces of toast and peanut butter and was working on a banana when Ryan began to yell again.

"Birdie!" he hollered. "Bad birdie."

"Birds are good," I told my little brother.

I turned to look outside. Jet was lying on the deck where I had left him, but something about his posture made me pay attention. Jet's ears were pricked straight ahead, and his face was cocked to the side.

Then I saw it. A small chickadee (probably a young and foolish one) had gotten impatient in the bird line. He had spotted several sunflower seeds that had fallen on the deck below the feeder. As I watched, the chickadee landed on the deck some distance from Jet and began to hop around, pecking at the wood.

Jet slowly raised his front end.

The chickadee hopped sideways and picked a seed up in its beak.

Jet exploded in a burst of black-and-white fur. He flew forward and tore awkwardly across the deck after the chickadee, barking loudly.

The chickadee escaped just inches ahead of Jet's open mouth.

Ryan began to cry and pounded the window again.

Jet stood there, his tail wagging wildly. It almost seemed that he had forgotten about his missing leg for a minute. He began to sniff the deck where the bird had stood, and then he carefully picked up a sunflower seed in his big white teeth. He began to eat the crunchy seed.

"You better go feed your dog," Dad said. He was grinning as he buttoned up his dress shirt. "Looks to me like he needs something to eat."

I didn't need to be told twice. I raced outside with a bowl of dog food in my hands.

Jet turned around when he saw me coming. He staggered slightly, then caught his balance and began to bounce toward me. His tail was still held cheerfully upright, and he didn't seem to be uncomfortable.

"Jet!" I exclaimed. I began to pet him again, a huge grin on my face. My dog was going to be OK! He was going to walk again—maybe even run.

Jet seemed pleased with himself, too. As I petted him the hum began. In a few minutes he was growling cheerfully while I scratched him all over.

Mom knocked on the window and motioned for me to come back inside. "Guess I'd better go," I told the dog. "Here, have something to eat." I pushed the bowl of dog food toward him.

Jet sniffed the food and looked at me. Then with a sigh he slowly began to eat.

"It's not as good as chickadee stew, is it?" I asked the little dog.

We were late for church. But by the time we walked out to the car, the dog food bowl was empty, and Jet was halfway across the yard, clumsily moving at a steady walk. It was a funny walk, like a dog on a pogo stick, but he was making progress.

A wonderful song like a church hymn welled up within me. I felt so happy I could have almost flown with the birds. Jet was going to get better. He was going to be able to walk and run and play!

And he was going to be happy again. That was the most important thing of all.

Grandpa and the Doghouse

Dad shook me awake early Sunday morning. "Time to get up, Mark," he said. "Your doghouse is calling!"

I groaned and rolled over in bed. "I don't hear a thing," I mumbled. "Can't it wait until later?"

Dad didn't answer; he just pulled the covers back.

With a sigh, I struggled out of bed and began to yank my clothes on. I had barely finished dressing when Dad swung my bedroom door open again.

"Rats!" he said. "I can't find my handsaw anywhere. And we'll need it for cutting wood."

"Ahhhhh!" I groaned with mock sadness. "That's just terrible!" I flopped back on the bed and pulled the blanket over me.

Dad frowned. "By chance, you haven't hidden the saw, have you, Mark?"

"Of course not," I said quickly. "But I have to admit that it would have been a pretty good idea."

Dad thought for a moment. "Well," he said finally,

"Grandpa Olsen's shed is full of tools. We'll just run over and pick up what we need from there."

I groaned and pulled the blanket all the way over my head.

Grandpa wasn't in his room when we stopped by the hospital to ask permission to borrow his saw. And he wasn't in the big dayroom watching TV, either. We finally found him in the craft room with a group of other men. Grandpa didn't see us at first, and both Dad and I stood for a minute, watching him work. Grandpa was carefully screwing two pieces of wood together. His hand trembled a little, but before long he was finished with one screw and had picked up another.

"Whatcha making, Grandpa?" I asked.

Grandpa's head snapped up, then he smiled at me. "Well," he said, "I see the Avon lady's back to visit me."

Several of the other men studied me carefully, eyebrows raised, but no one said anything.

"Grandpa!" I objected. "Everyone's going to think I'm some sort of nut."

Grandpa threw his hand out in a sweeping gesture. "Gentlemen," he said, "I'd like to introduce you to my grandson. And yes, he is some sort of nut!"

The men nodded at me, then turned back to their work.

"What are you building, Father?" Dad asked, looking over Grandpa's shoulder.

Grandpa shrugged. "Nothing too exciting. Only a birdhouse. The hospital thought it would be nice if we could attract birds for the old people to watch."

"We have a little project of our own going on today," Dad said. "Mark's going to be building Jet a doghouse."

I sighed deeply.

"But I can't find my saw," Dad continued. "I wondered if you'd mind if I ran over to the farm and picked up a few of your tools."

Grandpa nodded his head. "Sure," he said. "Help yourself. You know where everything's kept."

"Do you want to come out to our place?" I suddenly asked. "You're good at wood work, Grandpa. You could help me with Jet's doghouse."

"Oh, no, Mark!" Dad scolded. "This is your project, not Grandpa's."

Grandpa glared at Dad. "Robert Olsen," he said in a firm voice, "I've had a stroke, but I'm not a total invalid! And I'm quite capable of helping my nutty grandson work on a doghouse!"

Dad sucked in his breath. "Why—why sure!" he sputtered. "That would be fine. I just thought you would be too busy to help Mark."

"Busy!" Grandpa scoffed. "Listen, Rob, I'm looking for something to do. Give me a few minutes, and I'll be ready to go out to the farm with you."

"Why don't you let me drive out to the farm and pick up the tools you'll need," Dad suggested.

"Fine," Grandpa said. He set the birdhouse down and turned to the man who was sitting in a wheelchair across from him. "Harold," Grandpa said, "you're in charge of the birdhouses now."

Harold pushed his glasses up with one finger and nodded his head.

"And make sure you do a good job," Grandpa continued. "We don't want to disappoint the old people."

I looked at the group of men. All of them had gray hair and wrinkles, but I guess if they were healthy enough to be building birdhouses, they couldn't be too old.

I pushed Grandpa's wheelchair down the hallway and into his room.

"You sure timed that right," Grandpa said after we had shut the door behind us. "Those men haven't the faintest clue what to do."

"Neither do I," I admitted.

"I'll whip you into shape in no time," Grandpa said. He rolled over to his closet and pulled a shirt off a hangar.

"That's what I'm afraid of," I said warily.

Grandpa grinned and began to slowly unbutton the shirt he was wearing. I watched his awkward fingers for a minute, wondering if I should offer to help. But although he was slow, Grandpa managed to get himself dressed before too long. When he was finished he turned to look at me. "So how's that mangy mutt doing?" he asked.

"We've got him home," I said. "And he's doing pretty good."

"I know," Grandpa said. "Your dad phoned me yesterday and told me all about his bird chasing."

"Dad phoned you?"

"You do own a phone, don't you?" Grandpa asked. I sighed. "Of course we do."

"Well, that's good," Grandpa said. "I wouldn't want to live at a house that didn't have a phone."

I thought about that for a moment. "Are you coming to live with us, Grandpa?" I asked.

"Would that be all right with you?" Grandpa Olsen asked.

"Sure!"

"I'm a pretty good guest," Grandpa said dryly. "The nurses say that my snoring is slightly quieter than a jackhammer, and since they want to fatten me up a bit I get to eat all the dessert myself. Other than that I'm a great guy to have around!"

"Grandpa!"

He smiled again. "Seriously, Mark," he said, "the doctor told me that I can leave the hospital next week. I want to go to my house, but they say I'm not quite ready for that. So I'll have to move in with you."

"That's OK!" I said quickly. "We have lots of space for you."

"So I won't have to sleep with your dog?" he asked.

"That would probably be more enjoyable than sleeping with Ryan," I said. "At least Jet doesn't yell all night."

"Your dad said that Jet's moving really well

now. Why didn't you tell me that he'd had his leg amputated?"

I shrugged. "I don't know. I guess I didn't want to upset you."

"Upset me?" Grandpa asked. "Why, I might have felt better if I'd have known that I wasn't going to be the only one who limped at your house!"

"Grandpa Olsen!"

"Sit down, Mark," Grandpa ordered. "I want to be serious for a moment."

"What's the chance of that happening?"

"Fair to middlin'," Grandpa laughed, "but I'm going to try. Mark, I want to thank you for talking to me about God the other day."

I blushed a little. "I guess I opened my big mouth at the wrong time again."

"What do you mean?"

"Well, I know what I want to say," I said, "but sometimes it comes out all wrong. Especially when it's about important things like God."

"You didn't do too bad," Grandpa said. "And after you went home I got to thinkin'. I realized that if you could still believe and defend God after all the things that had happened to your dog, then you must really, truly believe. Most of the time I think Christians are just saying things that they've heard before instead of what's really in their hearts."

I kept my lips pinched tightly together, listening to Grandpa.

"You know," Grandpa went on, "I believe in God, too. And I've prayed more since my stroke that I ever have in my entire live. But sometimes it really doesn't seem like my prayers are going anywhere."

"I'm sure God is listening to you," I said quickly.

"Mark," Grandpa said, "I want to be like you. I'd like to trust God, even when things aren't going very well."

"Well, Grandpa, I don't have all the answers, either," I admitted.

Grandpa laughed. "If you told me you had all the answers, I wouldn't believe you," he said. "But maybe you could show me where to start reading in the Bible. Some of it looks pretty confusing to me."

"I'll help you, Grandpa," I promised.

Grandpa smiled. "I had an idea you'd say that. Now don't get all excited, or anything. Next thing I know, you'll be building a pulpit to stand behind and preach to me!"

I laughed. "Don't worry about that," I said. "I'm not going to build anything that I don't have to build!"

"Good," Grandpa approved. "Let's take things nice and slow. You can help me when I'm stuck in the Bible, and I'll tell you where you're all wrong!"

"Grandpa!"

"I don't want no preachers in fancy suits stopping by my house," Grandpa said. But his eyes twinkled at me like they used to do in the old days.

I couldn't stop myself. I sprang to my feet and grabbed Grandpa Olsen in a great big bear hug.

"Take it easy!" Grandpa said with a grunt. "You wouldn't want to knock an old coot like me right out of my wheelchair."

"I'm not that strong," I assured him, making a muscle with my right hand.

"You're strong enough, for a young pup," Grandpa said. "And speaking of pups, we better get ourselves in gear. Your dad's going to be here in a few minutes, and we're still not ready to go."

"Grandpa?"

Grandpa looked up. "What, Mark?"

I hesitated. "Will you do the hammering for me?" I asked.

Grandpa shook his head. "No way!" he said. "I'm just the supervisor. You work, and I yell!"

"Grandpa!"

"That reminds me of a joke I heard," Grandpa said, looking at me sideways. "Seems this farmer had a hired man helping him haul bales. The hired man was a big fellow, but he didn't like to work too hard. Every time they'd drive out to the field, the hired man would grunt and groan and grumble while the farmer ended up doing all the work."

I think I got a little red in the face. Had Dad been talking to Grandpa about our bale hauling earlier in the month?

"Anyhow," Grandpa continued, "the farmer finally turned to the hired man and said, 'Bill, let's get one thing straight. We have to work as a team. This time I

126

want *you* to do the work, and *I'll* do the grunting!'"

I laughed. "Grandpa! That's bad!"

"Well, that's what we're going to do with the dog-house," Grandpa said. "You're going to do the work, and I'll do enough grunting for both of us!"

"That's what I like to hear!" Dad smiled at us from the doorway. "Now come on, men. There's a certain three-legged dog at home who needs a place to live."

🦴 🦴 🦴

I guess that's where I'll end my story.

Jet's doing a lot better. Just last week he began to run around the lilac bush and jump after birds again. He doesn't get quite as high, and he sure can't move backward very quickly, but otherwise he manages fine. The chickadees have learned that they had bet-ter keep up in the air and off the deck if they don't want to be dog lunch.

Grandpa's supposed to be moving into our house in a few days. Mom's putting him in the bedroom next to me. I think that will be great, except I'm a little worried about his comment about snoring. Maybe he was just joking. I hope.

Grandpa and I have talked a bit more about God. I don't know if I've been any help to him, but I do know that he has a Bible on his hospital stand now. I figure that's a good start. I might be famous for saying the wrong things at the wrong time, but the Bible never does.

I love Grandpa Olsen.

And I love my worthless, no-good dog. He loves me, too. It had been a horrible winter for Marvelous Mark and his Mighty Moving Mouth. But things are looking up.

And I guess that's the way God wants it to be.